ABSOLUTELY,

POSITIVELY

NOT

GAY

DAVID LAROCHELLE

SCHOLASTIC INC.

New York Toronto London Auckland Sydney

Mexico City New Delhi Hong Kong Buenos Aires

ACKNOWLEDGMENTS

I am deeply indebted to the following people for their unfailing encouragement and support: Laurie Skiba, Gary Nygaard, Timothy Cope; the Delton Group: Kerin McTeigue O'Connor, Joyce Simon, Beth Voigt, Marge Peterson, Georgie Peterson; and the KTM writers: John Coy, Janet Lawson, Jody Peterson, Cindy Rogers, Phyllis Root, and Jane Resh Thomas. And special thanks to Arthur Levine, for his trust and faith when I was delirious with doubt.

Inspired by his story "Taking Alice to the Prom," which appeared originally in *Cicada* magazine.

ISBN-13: 978-0-439-59110-2
ISBN-10: 0-439-59110-4

Arthur A. Levine Books hardcover edition designed by Kristina Albertson, published by Arthur A. Levine Books, an imprint of Scholastic Inc., June 2005.

12 11 10 9 8 7 6 5 4 3 2 1   9 10 11 12 13 14/0

Printed in the U.S.A.   40
This edition first printing, April 2009

TO JUDY DELTON

CHAPTER ONE

Everybody has at least one ugly secret, and mine is as ugly as they come.

I square-dance.

With my mother.

I'm not talking once-a-year square dancing. I'm talking *serious* square dancing, every week, where the women wear fluffy checkered skirts that stick out a yard on either side and the men wear matching cowboy shirts and everyone wears a big plastic name tag shaped like a music note.

And the ugliest part of this secret is . . . I actually like it.

It's not the outfits, which make us look like escapees from a clown school. It's not the corny music either.

What I like about square dancing is that there's never any doubt about what to do. A promenade is always the same:

men on the inside of the circle, women on the outside, escort your partner until you come back to your home position. Do what the caller tells you, and you'll be just fine. And if you ever get confused, follow the other dancers. When we're all in perfect step with each other, it's like I'm part of a well-made machine. It's beautiful.

I realize this is the twenty-first century. Being a sixteen-year-old square dancer might be the sign of a serious social disorder. But the sorry truth is that square dancing makes me happy . . . at least as long as nobody else finds out about it.

CHAPTER
TWO

"Slow down, Steven, before you get us killed!"

My mother reached across the car and sank her fingernails into my forearm. Our family's Buick swerved dangerously toward the ditch. I had to twist the steering wheel back to the left to avoid flying off the road.

"Take it easy, Mom. I was only going the speed limit."

My mother's grip on my arm tightened.

"Speed limits are for experienced drivers, Steven. When you've had your license for six or seven years, then you can talk to me all that you want about speed limits. Right now you have a learner's permit, which means driving at a learning speed."

I eased up on the gas pedal until my mother's death grip

loosened. When she finally let go we were creeping along at 18 mph in a 30 mph zone.

"That's better," she said. "Don't you feel safer? Don't you feel like you have more control of the car?"

I felt like I was going to be late for school.

We crawled past City Park and the fifty-foot-tall fiberglass hockey stick proclaiming Beaver Lake, Minnesota, HOCKEY STICK CAPITAL OF THE WORLD. The Hat Trick Café and Bruce's Blue Line Bar & Grill lined the other side of the street. Just because the plant where my dad worked produced more hockey sticks than any other city in the country, the entire town of nine thousand was obsessed with the game.

I hate hockey.

We pulled into Beaver Lake Consolidated High at 7:28, two minutes before my first class.

I grabbed my backpack and scrambled out of the car.

"Don't forget we've got you-know-what tonight," called my mom. I had warned her against using the words "square dancing" while on school property. She slid over to take my place behind the steering wheel. "And you forgot your stocking cap! Do you want to get sick?"

I doubted whether sprinting the ten feet from the curb to the front entrance without a hat would result in pneumonia, but I scooped up my stocking cap anyway. The first-hour bell began ringing as I reached my locker. After grabbing the books I needed for the morning, I raced to my homeroom, dodging the few stragglers still in the hall. When I dropped into my front-row desk, I was only thirty seconds late.

My best friend, Rachel, leaned forward in her seat behind mine. "Riding with your mom again?" she asked.

I nodded, too out of breath to speak. Then I pulled a pocket notebook from the back of my jeans, turned to a fresh page, and printed "19 minutes, 12 seconds." That was how long it had taken me to drive from our house to school. My parents wouldn't allow me to take my behind-the-wheel test until I had clocked two hundred hours of practice with a licensed adult driver. Only eighty-three hours and twelve minutes left to go. With a little luck, I'd have my license before it was time to put me in a retirement home.

As I slid the notebook back into my pocket I realized we were missing our teacher. Even stranger, the blackboard was blank. Health class with Bud Corcoran never varied. For the first half hour we copied the meaningless notes covering the blackboard while Corcoran read the newspaper and drank coffee. For the second half hour Corcoran read the same notes aloud, word for word, while we studied for another class or slept. Most people slept. Our grade was determined by how many pages of notes we took.

I turned around to face Rachel. "Where's Corcoran?"

"In prison, for impersonating a teacher."

Rachel loathed the man. I was a little less critical. I was a good note taker, and the class was an easy "A."

A voice from the back row spoke up. "If Corcoran doesn't show in one minute, I'm out of here."

The prospect of starting the day with a free hour perked everyone up. Even the kids who had been slumped across their desks with closed eyes lifted their heads and started watching the clock.

Twenty seconds left. Ten. The room was silent as the skinny red hand ticked off the remaining seconds.

"Time's up!"

We all stood and gathered our books, then headed for the exit. Just as we were about to make our escape, the way was blocked by a tall, well-dressed man in his mid-twenties.

The class moaned.

"Fine way to greet your teacher," he said as we shuffled back to our desks.

Substitute.

I hate substitute days. Either the class rips the sub into tiny pieces, or the sub jumps all over the class like a grizzly. Neither is fun to watch. If I want to see carnage and bloodshed, I'll watch it on the Nature Channel.

The teacher scrawled "Bowman" across the blackboard in wide, relaxed letters, then tossed the tiny chalk stub across the room, where it landed in the wastebasket beneath the pencil sharpener. He lifted himself onto the edge of Corcoran's desk so that he was sitting directly in front of me.

"I regret to inform you that Mr. Corcoran was involved in a handball accident over the weekend."

Corcoran played handball? For the past two months I had never seen him move from the padded chair behind his desk. He rewarded students with extra-credit points for bringing him his lunch from the cafeteria.

"Some of you might know me as the new assistant hockey coach, but until your teacher is back on his feet again, I'll be helping with his class."

He picked up the thick three-ring folder labeled HEALTHY CHOICES FOR A HEALTHY YOU, which contained all of Corcoran's master notes. "Let's see what we've got on today's agenda."

He turned to the page marked with a bookmark and cleared his throat. "'The Importance of Chlorogenic Acid in a Young Person's Diet.'"

Mr. Bowman closed one eye and studied the page. I was the only one close enough to hear what he muttered: "What the hell is 'chlorogenic acid'?

"Forget that," he said, snapping the folder shut and hopping off the desk. He unbuttoned his cuffs and rolled up the sleeves over his muscular arms. He shook open the newspaper he had brought along and turned to the editorial page.

"'Fast-Food Franchises Responsible for Rising Obesity.'" Folding his arms across his chest, he studied the class. "True or false?"

Silence.

Well, what did he expect? It was first hour, Monday morning.

Most teachers would rather answer their own questions than listen to silence, but Mr. Bowman just stood there and smiled. It looked like we were in for a very quiet morning.

"True."

It was Rachel, behind me. She was a vegetarian and thought fast-food restaurants were evil.

"False," said someone on the other side of the room. "Nobody can make you eat anything you don't want to."

"Great!" said Mr. Bowman, rubbing his hands together. "We've got our two lawyers." He pointed to the back two rows of the class. "You're the jury. Everyone else is a witness for one side or the other. Lawyers, you have ten minutes to prepare your cases. Anyone who doesn't participate stays after school and washes jockstraps for the hockey team."

The threat of unwashed jockstraps got everyone moving. I was the only witness who volunteered for Rachel's side, and I was worried she would make me deliver a long speech about the perils of high-fat foods. To be honest, a plate of onion rings, a slice of pizza, and a Death by Chocolate donut was my idea of a gourmet meal.

"You won't have to say a word," she promised. "I'll do all the talking."

She laid me across Corcoran's desk and referred to me as Exhibit A.

"Observe, if you will, the effects of corporate advertising on a typical American."

She tapped my forehead with Corcoran's yardstick. "Brainwashed into believing that the more you eat, the happier you'll become."

She tapped my stomach. "Bloated, from a diet of greasy burgers, deep-fried french fries, and sugar-laden soft drinks."

She tapped my mouth. "Voiceless, against the powerful barons of the fast-food industry who rule the television and radio airwaves."

Despite my preference for the fats and sugars food group, I tend toward the scrawny side, so Rachel had stuffed my shirt with her backpack and some crumpled newspaper from the recycling bin. I let my tongue fall out of my mouth and tried my best to look appropriately unhealthy.

The opposing side's key witness stood on a desk and struck a Statue of Liberty pose. He began his rebuttal with, "I am proud to be an American who can eat and sell whatever food I choose, even if it gives me high blood pressure and kills me before I am thirty." Surrounding him, the other students placed their hands over their hearts and hummed a medley of fast-food jingles.

Perhaps I was biased, but I thought Rachel had made some pretty good points. Even so, the jury ruled against her, 10 to 2. She was protesting the decision and demanding the chance to take the case to a higher court when the bell rang.

"Class dismissed," said Mr. Bowman, pounding a stapler like a gavel. "Everyone gets an 'A.'"

We streamed out of class, joining the noisy crowd in the hallway making their way to their second hour.

"That was a welcome relief," said Rachel, stepping around a group of seniors holding an impromptu game of tackle football in the hall.

"But you lost the debate," I said.

Rachel didn't look too upset. "At least it kept me awake."

We reached the spot where Rachel and I parted ways until lunch.

"And besides," she said before she turned the corner, "I think Mr. Bowman is kind of cute."

She raised her eyebrows and waited for me to respond.

Cute?

Was Mr. Bowman cute?

Sure, he had thick black hair that was slightly mussed, as if he had just stepped out of a convertible. And true, he dressed in sharp-looking clothes that showed off his bodybuilder's physique. And yes, when he smiled, his sky blue eyes smiled as well, making it difficult to concentrate on anything else.

But did I think he was *cute*?

"I didn't notice," I said loudly, then quickly headed off to geometry.

CHAPTER
THREE

There is nothing wrong with a teenage boy noticing how a male teacher looks. I've been noticing my male teachers for years. I happen to be a very observant person. Being observant is a wholesome and admirable trait. Thomas Edison was observant. Galileo was observant. Nobody ever thinks there's anything strange about them.

How could I help but notice that Mr. Bowman was above average in the looks department? The guy was sitting less than two feet away! That doesn't mean that there's anything unusual about me. To think otherwise makes me laugh.

Ha!

Unfortunately, I wasn't very observant in geometry. As Mrs. Moe explained how triangle ABC was congruent to triangle ABD, my mind kept wandering back to Mr. Bowman's smile. And his arms. And his sharply creased dark gray cotton pants. Mr. Bowman was congruent to the best-looking guy on any late-night cable drama.

The morning went downhill after that. It was worm dissection day in biology. We were each given an earthworm and instructed to peel back its skin and identify its major organs. My worm was the width of a toothpick. It was all I could do to stab the thing with my scalpel, let alone split its skin evenly down the middle.

"You should have refused to do the assignment," Rachel told me at lunch. She took a bite of her hummus sandwich, and a lock of hair swung over her eyes. Rachel dyed this lock a different color on a regular basis. Today it was navy blue. "Dissection is cruel, Steven. Even on worms."

I poked a fork at a limp strand of school spaghetti lying on my plate, but couldn't make myself eat it. The pale yellow noodle looked disturbingly like a dying earthworm.

After lunch I had another acute attack of observation. It was when I spotted Mr. Bowman walking to the teachers' lounge. I observed him twice more that afternoon, standing outside Corcoran's door chatting with other students, and when I stopped by his room at the end of the day, just to make sure I hadn't missed any homework he might have assigned. He smiled when he saw me and remembered my name. Pretty observant on his part, after only one day of class.

If Mr. Bowman was so observant, why should I be concerned about my own highly developed observational skills?

■ ■ ■ ■ ■ ■ ■ ■

When I got home from school, I nearly tripped on a large cardboard box blocking the kitchen door. It was another shipment of my mother's best-selling book, *The Clean Teen: A How-To Manual on Raising Tidy Teenagers.*

I pushed the carton to the side of the room next to a stack of last month's newspapers. After searching behind the empty cereal boxes and dusty piles of junk mail on the counter, I finally found a candy bar left over from Halloween. A year ago. My mother claimed that if she worried about being immaculate herself, she'd never have time to write.

"Hi, Steven. How was your day?"

I passed the study where my mom was engrossed in her latest project, a cookbook for working women. My mother never cooks. It's my father who makes the meals at our house.

"Fine," I answered, stepping over a pile of dirty laundry and a bag of vacuum cleaner replacement parts.

When I reached my room I shut the door and stood for a moment, absorbing the tranquility of the only orderly spot in the house. Everything was folded. Everything was dusted. Everything was exactly where it belonged. My mother had trained me well.

After hanging up my backpack I climbed onto my bed, candy bar in one hand, geometry notebook in the other. I studied the notes I had scribbled in class, but it was hopeless. Nothing I had written all day made any sense.

I leaned back and stared at the ceiling. Carefully pinned above my bed was a poster of Superman in flight. I've been a Superman collector for years. In fact, my closet was a small, neatly labeled, thoroughly organized tribute to the world-famous Man of Steel.

I studied the poster for the millionth time. Mr. Bowman would make a good Superman. I pictured him in tights.

Dang!

I sat up, knocking my notebook to the floor.

So what? So what if I had been thinking about Mr. Bowman every five minutes all day long? That meant nothing. He was an interesting teacher, that's all. I bet every single one of his students was thinking about Mr. Bowman right this very moment.

Uneasily I lay back down on my bed.

There was no reason for me to be worried. It's not like I was gay. I knew what the TV evangelists said about gay people. I've heard the wisecracks in the locker room. You don't have to tell *me* about the nasty words people substitute for "homosexual." There is *nothing* gay about me.

I sat up again.

Except for maybe those magazines.

Beneath my bed, in a shoe box wrapped in rubber bands, locked in a suitcase covered with an old blanket, were two magazines: *The Men's Undergear Catalog* and *International Male*. I had discovered them at our neighbor's when she had asked me to take in her mail. I figured the post office had made a mistake. What was an eighty-year-old woman going to do with a catalog full of male models in thongs and jockstraps? Not wanting her to be offended, I had brought the magazines home with every intention of throwing them away. Two years later I hadn't gotten around to it yet.

So what?

Just because I occasionally flipped through those magazines late at night in the privacy of my bed, did that mean I was gay? What's wrong with wanting to be up-to-date on underwear fashions? Straight men wear briefs, don't they?

And just because I very infrequently stumbled across Web sites that showed pictures of naked men, did that mean I was gay? It's almost impossible to avoid those sites, no matter how hard you try.

I stood up and punched my pillow.

No! I was absolutely, positively not gay. What's more, I was going to prove that I wasn't.

I yanked the suitcase from under my bed, snapped open the locks, and pulled the rubber bands off the shoe box. Then I ripped the catalogs into tiny shreds until I was left with a pile of scraps no bigger than postage stamps. I stuffed the pieces into a plastic grocery bag, tied it tight, and carried it out to the trash where I buried it beneath the remains of last night's dinner. See! If that didn't indicate how *not* gay I was, what did?

"Case closed," I said, dropping the lid down on the garbage can.

I returned to my bedroom and slid my suitcase back where it belonged. Nobody could ever think that I was gay now. Because I wasn't.

I sat down on the edge of my bed.

Maybe I should get a tattoo. Something like a bloody skull, or a snake with daggers coming out of its eyes. Or better yet, a great big busty woman in a tiny bikini. It could cover my entire forearm.

When I went to my desk to get a ballpoint pen for sketching possible tattoo designs, a stray scrap of paper on the carpet caught my eye. It was a shred from one of the magazines, showing somebody's bare elbow or knee. It could have been a woman's knee if I didn't know any better.

Of course! That was it! I didn't need a tattoo. What I needed was something a lot less expensive and considerably less painful. What I needed was a *Playboy.* Guys who are gay do not keep *Playboy* magazines in their bedrooms.

What a simple and elegant solution! The magazine could be hidden beneath my mattress and pulled out whenever I needed a gentle reminder that I wasn't gay. And if my parents accidentally stumbled across it, so what? Nothing wrong with a sixteen-year-old boy satisfying his natural curiosity about girls.

It was only four o'clock. I could still do it before dinner. The sooner I got this whole gay issue settled once and for all, the better.

Five minutes later I was out in the cold, walking to Bart's Gas-O-Rama. It was a dumpy gas station–convenience store that catered to truck drivers. If there was one place in town that could be guaranteed to have adult magazines, this was it.

I stepped inside and huddled next to the snack area, trying to absorb some warmth from the heat lamps shining down on two ancient bratwurst. When I was thawed, I wandered to the back of the store where the magazines were kept. A quick purchase and I'd be heading home, confident in my heterosexuality.

"Why, hello, Steven! What a pleasant surprise!"

A gray-haired lady in a pink flannel coat was coming my way. It was Miss Abbergast, my first-grade teacher.

"Hi, Miss A."

I thought she had retired to Arizona.

"It's so nice to see you. How is school going? And how are your parents?"

Usually I like chatting with my old teachers, but not today. I was on an important mission with no time to be sidetracked.

"Are you getting gas, Steven?" It sounded like a question

about my digestive system. "I can't believe you're already old enough to drive."

"Actually, I'm here to . . ."

I'm here to buy a dirty magazine full of naked women in lurid poses.

". . . I'm here to pick up a few things for my mom."

I grabbed something from the nearest shelf. A dented can of olives.

Miss Abbergast smiled. "You were always one of my most thoughtful students. I'm glad to see that you haven't changed."

She brushed past me to the back of the store and parked herself next to the magazine rack. She picked up a copy of *The National Enquirer* and began to read.

As much as I wanted the world to know that I wasn't gay, I couldn't bring myself to buy the *Playboy* with Miss Abbergast standing right in front of it. While she worked her way through the latest celebrity gossip, I roamed the aisles and waited for her to leave.

For someone who taught so many kids to read, Miss Abbergast was a painfully slow reader herself. When the clerk behind the cash register began to eye me, I picked up a plastic shopping basket so I'd look like a serious customer and not some juvenile delinquent casing the joint for a shoplifting spree. Breath mints, a box of plastic forks, a can of WD-40. Soon my basket was full.

Miss Abbergast continued reading. She finished the *Enquirer* and moved on to *The Weekly World News*. The Pennzoil clock above the cash register said 5:43. My father puts dinner on the table at six and I've learned it's best not to be late.

Finally Miss Abbergast pulled a flowered head scarf out of her pocket and tied it over her hair. She picked up a copy of *Time* and headed for the cashier. "Tell your mother hello," she called, waving at me.

"Will do," I said, waving back.

The moment she was out the door I made my move before one of my old Sunday school teachers showed up.

The men's magazines were high on the top row. I set the shopping basket down and reached for the *Playboy*. My fingers were touching its cover when my eyes drifted to another magazine below. It showed a dark-haired, bare-chested man with a big grin. He could have been Mr. Bowman's brother.

Maybe I should check.

I slid the magazine out of the rack. The man on the cover was wearing nothing but a flaming red Speedo. "Sizzling Swimwear for the Man in Your Life," read the caption.

Come to think of it, I needed a new bathing suit. Better take a look.

"There's a ten-minute limit on reading, boy."

I shoved the magazine back. A grizzled old man half my size stood inches away, glaring like a bloodthirsty weasel.

The patch on the front of his oil-stained overalls said BART.

"I'm not reading, I'm buying."

I grabbed a different magazine and dropped it into my basket. Only then did I notice its title: *New Baby, The Magazine for Young Mothers.*

Bart narrowed his eyes.

"My girlfriend is pregnant," I explained. "I'm picking up a few things that she needs."

Like plastic forks and WD-40.

Bart smiled, showing more empty spaces than teeth. "We sell diapers too, you know. It's never too early to stock up."

I couldn't tell if he was being sarcastic or not. I bought a box of the extra absorbent.

The clerk rang up my purchases, wiping me out of every cent that I had. I ran to make it home by six.

"Dinner is on the table in five minutes," said my dad as I came into the kitchen. He glanced at the bag of groceries in my arm, and the ends of his bushy eyebrows met. Sticking out from the top of the bag were the disposable diapers.

"It's for an art project at school," I said. "You know, papier-mâché."

I hurried to my room before he could say anything else and leaned my back against the door. What a wasted trip. A lot of useless junk, and not the one crucial item I needed.

When I emptied the grocery bag onto my bed, the *New Baby* magazine landed on top of the pile. What was I going to do with *that*? I leafed through its pages and was about to toss it in my wastebasket when I spotted a full-page ad for Victoria's Secret. It seemed out of place among all the bassinets and teddy bears, but maybe new mothers were interested in looking sexy too.

The woman in the ad was wearing lacy black underwear and standing on a beach. She was staring seductively at the camera. Her lips were parted as if she were about to reveal her innermost desires.

Maybe my trip to Bart's wasn't a waste after all.

I carefully ripped the photo out of the magazine and carried it to my desk. I turned on my lamp and trimmed the torn edges with a pair of scissors. I cradled the picture gently in my hand. "You are so beautiful," I whispered to the photo. "You're everything I've always wanted in a woman."

I traced my fingers along her outline. I stroked the image of her cascading blond hair. I let my fingers linger on her breasts.

"Sexy, sexy, sexy. You must be the hottest babe in the world."

I closed my eyes and kissed the photo, leaving wet lip prints on the glossy paper.

"I'd do anything to have a girl like you."

The woman looked unconvinced.

I couldn't blame her. I didn't even sound convincing to myself. Even worse, when I had closed my eyes to kiss the photo, the image that had popped into my head was the bare-chested man in the Speedo.

I flicked off the lamp.

What was I doing wrong? Everyone knows that guys my age are supposed to be excited by pictures of women with big breasts. Why else would they constantly show women like that on TV?

I opened my desk drawer and pulled out a roll of tape. I taped the photo onto my wall, just below the framed copy of my favorite comic book cover: Superman flying off with a young man who's about to be flattened by a meteor. Maybe if I looked at this woman in her underwear long enough, I'd eventually find her arousing.

"Dinnertime, Steven! *Now!*"

I opened my bedroom door and the room filled with the smell of garlic from my dad's tomato sauce. Time to face another plate of spaghetti.

CHAPTER FOUR

"My god, Steven, you drive like an old lady."

My father reached over and planted his heavy hand on my knee and pressed down. The car accelerated and my head snapped back.

"I was only going the speed limit," I said.

"Nobody drives the speed limit," my father informed me. "Except maybe your mother."

We barreled through town, my hands clenched to the steering wheel.

"It's nighttime, Dad. Aren't you supposed to drive slower at night?"

The Beaver Lake hospital whizzed past us in a blur. If we crashed, at least the ambulance wouldn't have far to go.

"If you drive like you're afraid, Steven, you'll always be afraid to drive."

He flicked on the dome light and began reading his newspaper. If he sensed I was slowing, he reached over and pushed my knee back down.

When we reached the library I was drenched in sweat. Driving with my dad always felt like an extreme-sports competition; I was never certain if I'd finish the event alive.

I climbed from the car and my father slid across the seat.

"If you want to survive on the road, Steven, you've got to drive like a man."

With that, he was gone, off to meet his buddies at the Blue Line to watch hockey on their wide-screen TV.

I took out my pocket notebook and added another six minutes and seven seconds to my driving log. A big disadvantage of driving with my dad was that I clocked only half as much time as when my mom was the passenger. I checked my watch again. I had half an hour before my mom came to pick me up for our weekly square dancing.

The library was almost empty. Good. The fewer prying eyes to notice why I was here, the better. It had been a week since my failed attempt to get a *Playboy* and staring at the Victoria's Secret ad had not jump-started my interest in girls. In fact, Mr. Bowman was looking better every day. If I wanted to secure my position as a heterosexual, it was time to try another approach.

The library, I reasoned, was a good place to start. It's where I discovered in second grade that warts are not caused by talking back to your parents, as my mother had claimed. It's also where I learned the literal definitions of "bastard" and "bugger," favorite swear words of my dad. I hoped it could help me with this problem too.

I glanced over at the reference desk. A woman with arms the size of golf bags was ripping the back covers from discarded paperbacks. A sign on her desk read, ASK ME! I'M HERE TO HELP.

No, I didn't think so. This wasn't a subject I could talk to a stranger about, especially one who resembled a professional wrestler.

I sat down at the online catalog farthest from anyone else. The computer prompted me to enter my keyword.

Gay?

No. I wasn't gay. Absolutely not.

Straight?

The word "straight" always made me think of rulers and straight lines. I wanted a book that dealt specifically with my worries, not a geometry study guide.

Instead I typed a word that went right to the heart of my problem.

Sex.

I hit the return key, and the screen was filled with titles, each and every one screaming that three-letter word:

Sex After Sixty

Sex, American Style

Sex Among the Nomadic Tribes of the Southern Sahara

Dozens and dozens of sex books, and this was only the first of thirteen pages.

At that moment the gigantic reference librarian passed behind me, pushing a cartload of videocassettes. Had my computer sent out a signal informing her that I was looking up dirty titles? I leaned forward and pretended to have a coughing fit, cleverly concealing the screen with my body. When she disappeared into a back room, I resumed my search.

Most of the books sounded useless or downright bizarre, but at the bottom of the tenth page was a title that held promise: *Sex, Your Son, and His Future* by Dr. Trent Beachum.

Sex and my future. That's exactly what I was worried about.

I copied its call number onto a scrap of paper, then cleared the screen, leaving no incriminating evidence behind. Making a slow, casual approach to avoid drawing attention to myself, I located the book in a dim corner of the library.

It was a small paperback with yellowed pages. The faded photo on the cover showed a happy mother and father beaming at their son, who was doing his homework in front of the fireplace. They were all wearing cardigan sweaters knit by the mother. I could tell, because she was in the process of knitting another one, possibly for the beagle that was lying obediently next to their son.

All right, the book was old. So what? If this book could help me, I didn't care if it had been carved from a slab of stone. Besides, Trent Beachum had a list of credentials that took up half the back cover, including Doctor of Philosophy and Outstanding Citizen of Plainview, Utah. If you couldn't trust an Outstanding Citizen, who could you trust?

I carried the book to a study carrel hidden behind a plastic rubber tree and skimmed through the chapter titles: "The Difference Between Boys and Girls" . . . "The Wonders of Puberty" . . . "Let's Be Frank About Proper Hygiene" . . . then bingo! "The Question of Deviant Sexual Behavior."

My heart kicked into overdrive. Even though he hadn't specifically used the word "gay," I knew exactly what Dr. Beachum meant.

I turned to Chapter 4 and started reading.

Most boys develop a healthy interest in young ladies sometime during their early to mid-teens, but on rare occasions, this does not occur.

Trent had me pegged. I had come to the right place.

There is no reason why this should cause any concern.

My shoulders dropped three inches in relief. Maybe I was okay after all.

Unless, of course, your son is demonstrating mannerisms that might be deemed effeminate.

My shoulders tensed up again.

Be on the lookout for these warning signs:
#1: Does your son prefer the company of girls to boys?

A cold shiver crept up my neck. Rachel, my best friend, was a girl.

#2: Does your son participate in activities that are female in nature, such as playing with dolls or dancing?

I had two plastic bins in my closet filled with collectible Superman action figures. Were they considered dolls? Even if they were still sealed in their unbroken blister packs?

And dancing . . . I was going dancing tonight, with my mother!

#3: Does your son like to dress up in women's clothing?

At least I could answer no to that one.

Except . . .

One year for Halloween I had dressed up as Mrs. Briggs, the elementary school principal, complete with a big red wig and her trademark green eye shadow. Everyone had thought this was funny. Even the teachers had laughed. But maybe it wasn't funny. Maybe this was leading me down the path of deviant behavior. Why hadn't somebody warned me?

If you answered yes to at least one of these questions . . .

I had answered yes to all three!

. . . then you should be very concerned.

I was!

But don't despair.

Too late!

There is still hope.

Thank you!

You can still save your son from a life of loneliness and shame, but you must act now. . . .

Just then the sound of a familiar voice made me look up. I peeked around the rubber tree and saw Rachel. She was at the checkout desk returning a stack of romance novels. "Who says a feminist can't read Harlequin Romances?" she had told me.

Rachel's head barely cleared the stack of books on the counter. It was her height — or lack of it — that had drawn us together in the first place. In kindergarten Calvin Sprugg had nicknamed us Teeny and Weenie because Rachel was so short and I was so skinny. Whenever the teacher wasn't looking, Calvin mouthed, "Teeny-Weenie, Teeny-Weenie" until the day Rachel got fed up and threw his tennis shoes into the goldfish tank. The name calling had stopped, and Rachel and I had been best friends ever since.

I slammed shut the book I was reading.

What had I been thinking? There was nothing wrong with having Rachel for my friend. There was nothing wrong with dancing either. Heck, there wasn't even anything wrong with dressing up as a woman. The football team dressed up as cheerleaders every year as part of the homecoming talent show and nobody ever called *that* deviant behavior.

If Trent Beachum thought having Rachel for a friend was wrong, then he knew nothing about me. Nothing. Maybe if I hurried, I could stick his clueless book back where I had found it and catch Rachel before she left.

When I went to return the book, however, the aisle was

no longer empty. Standing where Trent Beachum's book belonged were two husky students from our rival, Lake Asta High. The backs of their letter jackets showed their mascot, the Fighting Walleye, and their sleeves were striped with yellow bars indicating all the times they had lettered.

Why weren't they at home watching hockey like everyone else?

I tucked Trent's book beneath my arm and kept my distance while I waited for them to leave. I hoped they'd browse faster than Miss Abbergast at the Gas-O-Rama.

"I don't know why we have to check out a *book*," complained one of them. "Why can't Hoffman let us watch a video instead?"

"Because she's a witch," said the other. "With a capital 'W.'"

I busied myself with straightening the books on the shelves and prayed that they'd find what they wanted soon.

"Hey! Look at the stupid faggot!"

I stopped straightening.

"Big deal. You want to marry him or something?"

"You bet. I'd like to marry him with a two-by-four up his —."

Suddenly there was no air. My chest tightened as if squeezed by an invisible fist.

It wasn't possible. I had been so careful. How could these guys know what I had been reading?

"Look at that faggy face! Losers like that make me sick."

I looked up and saw that the two had moved closer. One was waving a brightly colored book titled *Gay Youth Today*. The cover showed a smiling young man draped in a rainbow flag.

"What kind of fruit would read crap like this?"

The fist around my chest loosened. They weren't talking about me after all. They were talking only about a book.

I laughed out loud in relief.

The two stopped talking, and their heads swiveled in my direction.

"What are *you* laughing at, Scumface?"

The air was suddenly gone again.

"Are you talking to me?" I said, looking over my shoulder. "I'm not laughing. I'm not even remotely amused."

The one with the book raised it like a club and started coming toward me. I knew I should run, but my feet had grown roots. Where was that beefy reference librarian when I needed her?

The Lake Asta jock grabbed my collar. A giant zit on the end of his nose stared back at me like a big white eye. He shoved the book hard beneath my chin. "Maybe you were looking for this."

I was going to die. I was going to have my throat slit by a library book. I was going to go to my grave without ever getting my driver's license.

"Not me," I choked. "I don't want any book."

His grip on my shirt tightened. My minutes on this earth were numbered.

"Wow," I gasped. "That is so incredible. That is really, really incredible."

The three-eyed walleye glared hatefully at me, then took the bait. "What? What's so incredible?"

"Your jacket. Those stripes. Did you really letter nine times?"

He lowered the book and let go of my shirt. "Ten," he said, flexing his arms so I could get a look at his sleeves.

"Ten," I repeated. "Impressive."

He studied the stripes to make sure he hadn't miscounted.

"Damn right it's impressive. And it'll be twelve by the end of the year."

"Jake!" called his friend. "Let's get out of here. I found what we need for Hoffman's class — unless you're getting the fag book."

"Hell no," said Jake, sticking the book upside down on the shelf.

I flattened myself against the wall, and the two passed by.

"Go Walleyes!" I told them as they swaggered to the checkout desk.

And then I was alone.

It took me several minutes to recover from this brush with the afterlife. Then I realized I was still squeezing

Trent Beachum's book beneath my arm. I looked at the happy family on the cover.

So what if Trent had a few outdated ideas? His entire book couldn't be bogus, or else the library wouldn't own a copy — right? And I certainly didn't want to spend the rest of my life being terrorized by library thugs like Jake.

Absolutely, positively not.

I brought Dr. Beachum's book back to the study carrel and continued reading.

You can still save your son from a life of loneliness and shame, but you must act now before it is too late. By following these simple guidelines . . .

"Steven! There you are!"

It was my mother, dressed in her square-dancing outfit. Her ruffled red and white skirt with the six layers of petticoats stuck out from beneath her winter jacket like a satellite dish. Her hair was tied back in a bright red bow, and she wore matching low-heeled dance shoes.

I shoved what I had been reading deep into the branches of the plastic tree.

"I've been waiting for you out in the parking lot for the past ten minutes."

An old man at a study table stretched his neck to get a better look.

"I'll be there in a second," I said. "I just need a little more time. Alone."

"Well, make it quick. We don't want to be late."

My mother swished back to the exit, her skirt rustling against the bookcases and tables.

When she was gone, I retrieved Trent Beachum's book from the fake plant.

Now what? I didn't have time to finish reading his advice and from the way he talked, I didn't have a minute to lose.

My options were limited. Handing the clerk at the checkout desk a book titled *Sex, Your Son, and His Future* was out of the question. Way out.

Which left me with only one choice.

Steal the book.

I corrected myself. Not *steal*. Borrow. Borrow the book without using my library card. It wasn't stealing if I planned to return the book when I was through.

I hid myself behind a rack of CDs, lifted my shirt, and slid the book beneath the waist of my jeans. Then, very calmly, I walked toward the exit, reminding myself that I wasn't doing anything wrong. Libraries are meant to help us, I told myself. Don't act guilty. Librarians can smell guilt.

I was only a few feet from the door when the book began to slip. Just a little. I started taking smaller steps, carefully avoiding eye contact with anyone else. The old man from the study table was leaving too, and bumped me on his way out. The book slid a few more inches down my pants.

Keep cool, Steven. Just one more step and I'd be home free. I stretched my arm and my fingers touched the door handle. I pushed the door and—

BEEP! BEEP! BEEP!

Piercing red strobe lights flashed above the door. A warning alarm screamed into my ears. The handful of people still in the library turned to stare.

The book in my pants had triggered the security system.

The killer reference librarian came charging like a rhino. I tried to think of a good reason as to why I had a sex book down my pants, but my brain refused to work. Scowling, she flicked a switch alongside the door and the alarm stopped, replaced by a pulsating silence. I crossed my legs and hoped she wouldn't notice the squarish bulge just above my right knee.

She wagged her head and frowned. "I am so sorry. That thing has been acting up all day. We've got a repairman coming tomorrow, but I should have kept the darn thing turned off."

Was she bluffing? Was she giving me one last chance to confess before calling the cops?

"I'm sorry if it scared you. Are you okay?"

"Me? Yeah, I'm fine."

I was on the verge of going into cardiac arrest.

She held the door open for me.

"I apologize again. Have a good evening."

I nodded like a bobble-head, then sidestepped into the night. Grasping my pants leg, I lowered myself into the driver's side of our car.

"I don't see any books," said my mom. "You made it sound like going to the library was an emergency. Did you find everything you wanted?"

"I'm not sure," I said.

As I drove us to the Sandville VFW, where we danced, I was careful not to make any sudden movements that might cause the book to drop to the floor. I drove slowly and cautiously, gently touching the accelerator, gently applying the brakes. I never came close to the speed limit. When I pulled into the VFW parking lot, my mother looked at me with admiration.

"That was excellent, Steven. I've never seen you drive better. I do believe you're learning."

CHAPTER FIVE

While my mom was getting out of the car, I shook Trent Beachum's book from my pants and stashed it beneath the driver's seat where I could retrieve it later. My dance clothes were folded in a neat pile in the backseat and I carried them into the VFW hall, where I changed in a cramped stall in the men's bathroom. Then I went downstairs to the dance floor, where the Busy Bees were gathering.

My mother first brought me to the Busy Bee Square Dancers when I was twelve. She had read a magazine article claiming that square dancing added ten years to a person's life. "I'd rather die young if I have to dress like an idiot," was my father's response when she bought him a red and white checkered cowboy shirt. Not discouraged, my mother exchanged the shirt for a smaller size and drafted me to take his place.

From my very first dance I felt right at home with the Busy Bees. They treated me like an adult, and I liked that. Nobody ever pinched my cheek or told me that I looked cute or talked to me in that phony, high-pitched voice that most people use with little kids. I was simply another dancer.

"Howdy, Geezer!"

Morris and Mavis Swenson spotted me coming down the stairs. Because I was the youngest member of the Busy Bees, "Geezer" had been my nickname almost from the start.

"We didn't see you when your mother arrived," said Morris. "We were afraid you weren't coming tonight."

"Heaven forbid I'd be stuck dancing with this old crank all evening," said Mavis, squeezing her husband's arm.

A few of the dancers were my mother's age, but most of the Busy Bees were like the Swensons, well into their denture-cream years. Age spots, hearing aids, and thinning hair were almost as much a part of their outfits as the brightly colored Western wear.

"Pretty good crowd tonight," said Morris.

Morris and Mavis were King and Queen Bee, the elected goodwill ambassadors whose duties included welcoming first-timers. My mom and I had finished a close second in the last election. Thank goodness runners-up did not have to wear official Busy Bee sashes across our chests like the Swensons.

"We're still looking for a few more dancers," announced Hank, our caller for the evening.

"Would you do me the honor?" I asked Mavis, offering her my arm.

She slipped her bony elbow through mine. "See how a gentleman acts?" she told her husband.

"Now don't you go spoiling her," said Morris. "Remember, I'm the one who has to live with her the other six days of the week."

Morris went to scout out the platters of cookies and brownies on the refreshment table while Mavis and I joined the others already on the floor.

"How you doin', Geeze?" called Hank as we took our place with three other couples. His voice was amplified by the speakers on either side of the room. He adjusted his headset, then blew into the mike to test its volume. "Looks like we've got ourselves a couple of squares. Rev up your engines, everybody, and let's start dancing!"

He leaned down and pushed a button on the portable CD player at his feet. A bluegrass version of "The Lion Sleeps Tonight" began to play.

"In the jungle, the mighty jungle, the lion sleeps tonight.

Bow to your partner, and bow to your corner, then swing her with all your might."

Hank's deep bass voice bounced off the display cases of WWII photos and military medals that lined the basement walls. His long ponytail swung to the rhythm of the upbeat music. His voice was strong and clear and always easy to follow.

Mavis and I moved from one familiar pattern to the next. We Boxed the Gnat, Slipped the Clutch, and See Sawed. Forward, backward, left, and right, the eight dancers in our square wove in and out of each other. As Hank and the music moved us across the floor, I forgot about Jake and his buddy at the library. I forgot about Trent Beachum's book and the reason why I needed it. I was just plain happy to be dancing with the Bees.

The dance lasted about five minutes. When the music ended, we all reached into the square and shook hands, thanking everyone else. Very civilized.

"Looks like we've got a newcomer tonight," said Mavis as we walked off the floor.

I followed her gaze across the crowded basement to where a tall, dark-haired man was talking to Morris. His back was to me, but I recognized him instantly.

It was Mr. Bowman.

Mr. Bowman in a hunter green cowboy shirt and a black leather vest.

"Geezer! Mavis! I have someone I want you to meet!"

I was suddenly overcome with the urge to dive beneath

the refreshment table and disintegrate into tiny subatomic particles. No one from school could be allowed to see me here.

Yet part of me wanted to gallop across the room and join them. It was, after all, Mr. Bowman, making Western wear look better than I ever thought possible.

Disintegrate or gallop? A tough call.

Mavis made the decision for me and pulled me toward her husband.

Remembering that I was the Vice King Bee, I rallied my manners and spoke first. "Hi, Mr. Bowman."

"It's Tom," he said, reaching out and shaking my hand with both of his. "This isn't school."

"You two know each other?" asked Morris.

The hand that Mr. Bowman had shook hung loosely at my side, feeling incredibly light.

"Steven is one of my star students, the only one to turn in extra credit four times last week."

I felt my face grow warm with pride.

"Your teacher's been telling me he's an old hat at square dancing."

"Every week, before I moved to Beaver Lake," said Mr. Bowman. "Square dancing runs in our family."

Not only were Mr. Bowman and I both keenly observant, we were both seasoned square dancers. It was amazing all we had in common.

"What about your wife?" asked Mavis. "Does she dance?"

Another famous Bowman smile. "I'm happily single."

People were gathering in the middle of the room and Hank was calling for more couples. Mr. Bowman extended his arm.

"Would you care to dance?"

For the tiniest fraction of a second, I thought he was talking to me.

"I'd love to," said Mavis.

As I watched the two walk off, my mother stepped up to my side. "This next dance is mine," she said, and dragged me into Mr. Bowman's square.

Usually my mom and I make a pretty good pair, but tonight I danced like a lame toad. I faced the wrong way. I swung the wrong partner. I moved the wrong direction. Hank had to interrupt his calling several times to give me individualized instructions: "It's a *Right*-Hand Chain, Geeze. Use your *other* right hand."

Nobody else in our square seemed bothered by these mistakes. Not my mother, not Mavis, not Mr. Bowman. When I ended up on the wrong side of the square, my mother just called, "I'm over here, Steven!" and everyone laughed good-naturedly.

I wanted to scream. The harder I tried to keep in step, the more I stumbled. It was as if someone had tied bowling balls to both of my legs.

Mr. Bowman, on the other hand, was smooth and relaxed. He was always exactly where he should be. He laughed with Mavis as he promenaded her around the square. When the men met in the center for a Right-Hand Star, his grip on my wrist was strong and confident.

I didn't dance again that evening. I had already humiliated myself once in front of Mr. Bowman, no need for a repeat performance.

Mr. Bowman, however, didn't miss a single dance. In fact, so many women wanted to be his partner that they eventually had to start a waiting list. And whether he danced with Mavis or my mother or Mildred Rademacher (who couldn't even do a Courtesy Turn without stepping on her partner's foot), Mr. Bowman never failed to look graceful and suave.

I observed him intently the rest of the night. Observation is a great way to improve your dancing skills.

When the final song had ended, Mr. Bowman came over and told me good-bye.

"Great to see you, Steven. I appreciated finding a familiar face."

He wasn't even sweating. After two hours of dancing, I was usually wetter than a fish.

"See you in the morning," he said.

The morning meant school.

All of my fears returned. What if Mr. Bowman announced to our class that he had seen me square-dancing in a VFW basement with my mother? What if he let slip that my nickname was "Geezer"? What if the school discovered I was a second-in-command Bee?

How many panic attacks could a teenager survive in one night?

Then again, maybe I had nothing to feel panicky about. Maybe Mr. Bowman wouldn't say a word. Maybe he was a closet square dancer just like me.

▪ ▪ ▪ ▪ ▪ ▪ ▪ ▪

"Watch for deer, Steven," warned my mother as I drove us home that night. "They jump out at you when you least expect it."

I turned on the high beams in case any suicidal deer were planning to leap out in front of our car.

"That was a pleasant surprise, meeting your teacher. He seems very nice."

"He *is* very nice," I said.

"And he's a wonderful dancer," she said.

"I agree. Totally."

"And he's such a handsome man," she said.

I sat up straighter and scanned the road for deer.

"I didn't notice," I said loudly.

CHAPTER
SIX

My parents were asleep. A towel was beneath my door to prevent any telltale light from escaping. My wastebasket was leaning against the door to serve as a warning signal in case someone tried to enter. I hadn't been this secretive since . . . well, two weeks ago, when I was poring over the underwear catalogs.

I switched on my flashlight and pulled Trent Beachum's guide out from under my mattress.

Most boys slip into deviant sexual behavior simply because they lack the proper male role models. This situation can be easily remedied, and should be done so at the first opportunity. Enroll your son in a sports program. Enlist him in Boy

Scouts. Encourage him to spend time with masculine young men whose behavior you would like him to emulate.

This was not good.

I hated sports. Not that I hadn't given organized athletics a fair try. In fact, when I was six I had been an active participant in a peewee hockey league for, oh, about twelve minutes. Bundled in my protective gear and strapped into my skates, I had wobbled two steps onto the ice and fallen on my face. I cried. Someone helped me back onto my feet. I fell on my butt. I cried. Someone helped me back onto my feet again. My helmet fell off, I fell on my face, I got a bloody nose. I cried. This time they didn't even bother helping me back onto my feet, they just carried me off the ice.

I never went back. The only reason I had wanted to join in the first place was because Rachel was on the team. When she learned that I had quit, Rachel quit too. We started a stuffed animal club together instead.

As far as Scouting, I had lasted a little longer: two weeks.

My father had signed me up after my cousin Bernard achieved the rank of Eagle Scout.

"We'll show him," my dad had said.

At my first Scout meeting I had sat next to Mrs. Dalton, our troop leader, and quietly worked on my craft project while the other boys ran around the Dalton living room throwing couch cushions at their Chihuahua. When I showed

Rachel the log cabin coin bank I had made out of Popsicle sticks, she wanted to join the Scouts too. Mrs. Dalton looked rattled when I brought Rachel along to the next meeting. She took the two of us aside and politely explained that if Rachel really wanted to be a Scout, she should join the Girl Scouts. Rachel politely explained to Mrs. Dalton that girls could be anything they wanted, and that she wanted to be a Boy Scout, and if Mrs. Dalton tried to stop her, Rachel would take her to court for sexual discrimination. Rachel was eleven years old at the time.

Not wanting to see Mrs. Dalton in jail, and not wanting Rachel to spend all of her allowance on lawyers, I decided to quit. Rachel and I started a recycling club together instead.

Sports were out. Boy Scouts were out. There had to be another way for me to spend quality time in the company of masculine guys my age.

The opportunity presented itself the next day in the cafeteria.

The morning had started on an especially good note: Mr. Bowman said nothing about our shared interest in square dancing, and he wore an open-collared shirt that showed off a tiny patch of his chest hair.

Then, while waiting in the hot-lunch line, I noticed Dwayne, the senior in front of me. Dwayne was the size of a refrigerator, the kind that is wide enough to store an entire cow. He wore black gym shorts pulled over a pair of gray sweats. The red lettering on the back of his T-shirt read, GIVE BLOOD — PLAY HOCKEY.

This was exactly the kind of guy Trent Beachum wanted me to hang out with. Tough, strong, masculine. I could smell the testosterone reeking from him, or maybe it was just his manly deodorant.

I watched as he ordered a double lunch, then walked to a table reserved for the hockey team at the far corner of the lunchroom.

There was one empty seat left at the table.

I should do it. I should walk right over there, swing my leg over the seat, and plop myself down. It was exactly what Trent Beachum would advise.

So what was stopping me?

Fear. Terror. Common sense.

I gritted my teeth and pushed those feelings aside. What did my emotions matter when my entire future was at stake?

I took one step in that direction. *Attaboy, Steven, keep it up.* I took another step. The rest of the lunchroom became a blurry hum as I focused on the table filled with the school's biggest and brawniest. I took the long way, partly to give me time to build up my courage, and partly to avoid the table where Rachel was waiting for me. I'd explain my absence to her later.

The closer I got, the bigger and louder these guys became. They overflowed their seats. They thundered like elephants. I quivered like a bread crumb in front of a vacuum.

A few feet short of their table, I stopped. If I invaded their territory, I'd likely be picked up, slammed to the floor, and kicked around a bit before being tossed headfirst into the garbage barrel. Was it worth it?

The memory of Jake's threats in the library pushed me forward. A friendly toss in the garbage had to be a lot less painful than a two-by-four up the rear end.

As I sat down and unfolded my napkin, Dwayne turned on me. He was wearing a Marlboro baseball cap. It was against school policy to wear advertising for tobacco companies, but I wasn't about to point this out to him.

"What do *you* want?" he growled.

Keep calm, Steven. You handled the Lake Asta militia, you can handle Dwayne.

"Nothin', man," I said. "I'm just hangin'."

Dwayne snarled and turned back to his friends.

A spark of excitement raced down my back. Trent Beachum had been right; only five seconds in their presence and I was already sounding like a good ol' boy in a beer commercial. Think how rugged I'd sound if I survived the entire lunch!

Munching my corn dog, I carefully studied how these jocks interacted with each other. Being as observant as

I am, I quickly discovered three distinct traits about my tablemates:

They hit each other a lot.

They swore a lot.

They belched a lot.

Dwayne pushed his hand into the face of the guy sitting across from him and belched, "Asshole!" All three traits in one smooth, unified gesture.

Boy, did I have my work cut out for me. Even Rachel's little sister was a better burper than I was.

After a few minutes, I noticed that the guys had quieted down. Something was happening in the middle of the table. I leaned around Dwayne to see what it was.

Someone had opened a milk carton, and the crew at the table was cramming scraps of food into it. Rachel sometimes compacted her garbage like this so the trash would take up less space in a landfill, but I doubted whether these guys were so environmentally conscious. Maybe they were constructing a food bomb. I hoped that I wasn't their intended target.

"Hey, do you want to get in on this?"

A burly guy with a shaved head and a Chicago Bulls sweatshirt was looking at me.

"Sure," I said. Trent Beachum would have been proud of how eagerly I was embracing the macho lifestyle.

"Hand over five bucks."

Five bucks to become a member of the most elite male society at school seemed like the bargain of a lifetime. I took a five-dollar bill from my wallet and handed it to the Bull, who added it to a pile of crumpled bills already on the table.

"Now put whatever you want into the milk carton."

Fearing it might be a trap, I cautiously asked why.

The Bull pointed to another hockey player. "Carp is going to drink it."

Carp was a shaggy-haired guy with friendly black eyes and a nice-looking wide mouth and—

I caught myself before I became too observant.

"But no skagging. Carp doesn't drink any skags."

Even the word "skag" sounded manly. I vowed to work it into my conversation at least three times by the end of the day.

"If he drinks it all without hurling, he keeps the money."

Someone shoved the milk carton down to my end of the table. It was already brimming with a thick stew of milk, chocolate pudding, vegetables, and bread crusts. A starving pig wouldn't agree to drink all that.

"Go on, stick something in," said the Bull.

I picked a raisin from my muffin and dropped it into the mixture.

The Bull snorted, then passed the carton to Dwayne,

who folded the top shut, held it over his head, and shook it vigorously. He handed it to Carp, who opened the top, raised it as if making a toast, and brought it to his lips.

"Chug! Chug! Chug!" chanted the men at my table, pounding their fists and sending my silverware rattling like wind chimes.

And chug is exactly what Carp did. I watched as he drained the carton, his jaws chewing while his Adam's apple bobbed up and down. Without stopping to breathe, he tilted his head farther and farther back. The chanting crescendoed into a roar.

Wham!

He slammed the empty carton down and the table cheered.

"Mouth check!" they called.

The human garbage disposal stood up and leaned across the table toward me, his black eyes ablaze with delight. Placing his nose only an inch from mine, he let his jaw drop and pressed his cavernous mouth closer for me to inspect. Other than fleshy bits of green and yellow food stuck between his teeth and a fuzzy white coating covering his tongue, his foul-smelling mouth was empty.

He snapped his mouth shut and raised his hands in triumph.

I wasn't so victorious.

I felt it coming. I tried to stop it. But I couldn't. I

opened my mouth and lost my lunch all over the top of my cafeteria tray.

"Gross!"

"Rude!"

"I'm out of here!"

By the time I had wiped my mouth with a napkin, everyone had fled, leaving me with a table covered with lunch bags, fruit rinds, and half-eaten sandwiches.

"You animals have really outdone yourselves today."

It was one of the hairnetted lunchroom ladies.

"Don't even think about leaving until you've cleaned up this mess that you and your buddies have made."

She dropped a wet, gray washrag that smelled of sour milk and ammonia in front of me. I picked up the cold rag and began wiping slop into an old plastic ice-cream bucket.

I couldn't have been happier.

In only thirty minutes I had convinced the lunchroom lady that I was a regular guy, just like all these other jocks.

CHAPTER SEVEN

I missed you at lunch."

It was the end of the day and Rachel was leaning against my locker, waiting for me.

"Uh . . . I was sitting with some new friends."

Rachel slid over so I could work my lock. "I noticed."

I twisted the dial right, left, right. "I hope you don't mind," I said.

I gave the lock a hard yank and—shoot. I never got the thing open on the first try.

"You can sit wherever you want, Steven. Those guys just didn't seem like your type. Why the sudden interest in hanging around hockey players?"

I gave the dial on my lock a couple of spins and started over. Right, left, right. Yank.

Nothing.

"Maybe I've decided to become more athletic," I said.

Rachel rolled her eyes. "Yeah, right. And I've just been elected spokesperson for Burger King."

Why was it so hard for her to believe that I could possibly be a jock? Sure, Rachel had helped me burn my gym uniform when I passed my freshman year of mandatory high school P.E., but maybe my tastes were changing. Even though she was my best friend, there were a lot of things about me that Rachel didn't know.

On the third try I finally got my locker open. Rachel watched while I organized my books for tomorrow.

"So, is your stomach any better?"

She hadn't missed a thing at lunch.

"Yeah. I think it was just one of those twenty-five-minute flus." I cleared my throat a couple of times. "Although I still have the urge to skag now and then."

Rachel hiked her books higher on her hip. "Well, I'm glad you're recovering," she said. "Give me a call tonight, unless you're too busy skagging."

She walked off to her locker and I shut the door to mine.

There's no law saying that you have to tell your best friend everything. True, Rachel was one of the few people who knew about my square dancing, but I was still entitled to a couple of secrets, especially if they concerned sexual realignment.

I returned to the hockey table the next day, a little worried that the team might react to me with hostility, considering my lack of stomach control. My fears, however, were completely unfounded. Nobody tossed a single negative word my way.

They simply ignored me.

Not a problem. I could deal with being ignored. Lack of attention never gave anyone a cracked rib or bloody nose.

Silent and unnoticed, I continued to eat at their table, carefully observing their behavior and dutifully incorporating it into my own. I taught myself to burp. I swore whenever I remembered to. I even began wearing a baseball cap around school. It was one my grandmother had mailed me from her recent trip to Branson.

At home I surrounded myself with a harem of female photos. No need to fork out the money for *Playboy*; these pictures were available everywhere for free. In *TV Guide*, in travel ads, even on my mother's box of bran flakes. Soon my Superman posters were buried beneath dozens of women in skimpy bikinis and lacy lingerie. The sexiest of these pictures I taped to the outside of my notebooks so that everyone at school would know I was a typical teenage boy brimming with girl-crazy hormones.

And soon, I knew, I would actually find these pictures appealing. According to Trent Beachum, it was only a matter of time. Hang out with the hockey players, absorb their influence, develop an attraction to girls.

In the meantime, I thought about Mr. Bowman a lot more often than I'd ever admit.

▪ ▪ ▪ ▪ ▪ ▪ ▪ ▪

It might be today.

I entered the cafeteria with a sense of expectation.

My breakthrough might come this very afternoon. The noise issuing from the hockey table was louder than usual, which I hoped was a positive sign. Maybe the team was involved in a previously unobserved male ritual, one that might be influential enough to awaken my sluggish interest in girls.

I hurried through the line, eager to join my comrades. It had been over a month since I joined their table, and Trent Beachum had promised that repeated exposure to —

I stopped a few feet short of my spot.

My reserved seat was no longer vacant.

Sitting at my place was Solveig Amundson, our school's petite Norwegian exchange student. The hockey players surrounding her were going off the deep end. They shoved each other onto the floor. They rolled up their sleeves to reveal their biceps. They howled and hooted and made every crude noise imaginable.

Solveig was fascinated. She covered her face in mock horror when the Bull fell from his seat. She swooned as

Dwayne smashed his opponent's arm to the table in an arm-wrestling match. She giggled at all of their stupid noises.

To put it mildly, the scene was disgusting.

I shifted on my feet and waited for her to leave.

She didn't.

Instead, she picked up a Tater Tot from her cafeteria tray and held it out to the team. "How you say . . . ?" she asked.

When one of the guys told her, she laughed as if it were the punch line to the funniest joke in the world. Dwayne, the Bull, and the rest of the guys around her laughed too.

I didn't laugh. I stared at the place where I should have been sitting. A lot was riding on my continued proximity to these men. Specifically, my future happiness.

For the first time in weeks my presence was noted by one of the team. The Bull spun around and glared at me like I was cow manure. "Get the hell out of here, Upchuck. Now!"

This couldn't be happening. My lunching companions wouldn't really abandon me, would they?

"I said scram, you homo."

It was as if he had kicked me in the gut with a boot.

Couldn't he see my baseball cap? Hadn't he noticed the photos plastered to my notebooks? What had I done — or not done — to make him think that I might be gay?

The Bull turned back to Solveig. I backed away and retreated to a table as far from their cross-cultural merriment as possible.

"Damn!"

I said it loudly and with great conviction. Then I let rip the most repulsive belch ever heard in the halls of Beaver Lake High.

Nobody around me even looked up.

For the rest of the lunch period I pulverized my Tater Tots with a fork until they had turned to a sticky, inedible mess.

* * * * * * *

All afternoon I kept replaying the Bull's remarks. Big mistake on my part. Instead of reliving my lunchroom Waterloo, I should have been paying attention to where I was walking.

"Ooof!"

The door to the Industrial Arts room flew open and nailed me squarely in the face.

I reached up and touched my nose. It was tender, but still in one piece. Then, above my lip, I felt the wet, sticky trickle of blood.

Mr. Pangborn, the I.A. teacher whose door had walloped me, stuck his bald head into the hallway. He examined my face and frowned.

"Great. Another bleeder."

Accidents involving blood loss were obviously a frequent occurrence in his class.

"The nurse's office is around the corner," he said. "She'll handle you. That's her job." He closed his door and called from the other side. "And for cripes' sake, try not to get blood on anything else or that will be another fifty forms I'll have to fill out."

"I'll do my best," I said through a pinched nose, then tilted my head back and slowly began feeling my way down the hall.

"Ooof!"

I walked smack into somebody's chest.

Mr. Bowman's.

"Steven, what happened?"

I sniffed a drop of blood back up my nostril. "I was ambushed by a door."

Mr. Bowman scratched his chin thoughtfully. "I've always felt that doors were a lot more dangerous than most people realize. Let's find a sink and get you cleaned up."

He steered me into the nearest boys' bathroom where I splashed cold water onto my face and washed the blood from my upper lip. He then handed me a damp pad of towels to hold against my nose. "How does that feel?" he asked.

The only thing I felt was the weight of Mr. Bowman's hand resting on my shoulder. "It feels pretty good," I said.

I could have stood there for hours; eventually, it became clear that my nose had quit bleeding. Mr. Bowman gave my shoulder a gentle squeeze. "A bloody nose is a good initiation into hockey, Steven."

"I've heard that," I said.

"You should consider going out for the team next year."

"I'll give it some serious thought."

He took a black marker from his pocket and wrote me a late pass on a clean paper towel. "Stay clear of those hostile doors," he advised as he walked off toward the office.

The pleasant floating feeling that always accompanied being around Mr. Bowman lingered for a moment, then reality took its place. A solid month at the hockey table hadn't done me a shred of good. I still wasn't attracted to girls. My peer group of masculine role models had ruthlessly rejected me. What was I supposed to do now?

Fortunately Trent Beachum was ready with the answer.

CHAPTER EIGHT

If your son continues to have sexually deviant thoughts despite plenty of positive interaction with male peers, you may very well be feeling frustrated.

You got that right, Trent.

There is, however, one last remedy that can work wonders in extreme cases: aversion therapy.

I was already familiar with aversion therapy from a science program I had seen on PBS. By zapping laboratory rats with a few thousand kilowatts of electricity every time they approached a slab of cheese, scientists had trained them to prefer the taste of freeze-dried lima beans over fresh cheddar. Amazing, but true.

Luckily Trent Beachum's approach did not require hooking me up to electrodes.

Place a sturdy rubber band around your son's wrist. Whenever an impure thought enters his brain, he should firmly and immediately give the rubber band a quick, sharp snap. Pain will soon lead to pleasure as your son learns to replace immoral desires with healthful ones.

Dr. Beachum never explicitly spelled out his definition of immoral desires, but fantasies about being an assistant at an *Undergear Catalog* photo shoot probably qualified in his book.

The next morning after breakfast I took the rubber band that had been wrapped around the newspaper and slipped it over my wrist. I pulled it back as far as it would go and gave it a practice snap.

Yow!

Trent had the pain part right. I hoped the pleasure half of his theory held true as well.

Since neither of my parents was available to take me to school, I was left riding the bus. When it arrived, I stepped inside the warm vehicle and nodded at Garth, the driver. He nodded back. Garth was an amateur Golden Gloves boxer and was wearing his faded muscle shirt from Vinnie's Gym and a pair of torn jeans.

SNAP!

I sat down. A freshman in front of me was reading the sports section of the paper. Over his shoulder I spotted a photo of two guys in a locker room giving each other bear hugs.

SNAP!

I turned my head toward the window. We passed a billboard for Calvin Klein underwear.

SNAP!

I closed my eyes. The guys across the aisle were talking about hockey. "If we make it to the state tournament, Coach Bowman says we can throw him in the showers."

SNAP! SNAP! SN—

The rubber band broke. I was less than three blocks from home.

Fortunately, sitting behind me was Bree Caruthers, sophomore class president, Student of the Month, and Miss Teen Hockey Stick from Beaver Lake Hockey Days. She was also a walking office supply store.

"Bree, could I borrow a rubber band?"

She punched an entry into her electronic date book and flipped it shut. "Of course," she said. She reached into a backpack the size of a steamer trunk. "Which would you prefer: pink, mauve, or blue?"

"Blue," I said. Blue was a man's color.

She handed me a wide blue rubber band and I stretched it over my fingers. I rolled it down to my wrist and carefully smoothed the rubber so it lay flat and even, just below the wrist bone. I gave it several tugs to test its strength.

"Good," I said. "Nice and sturdy."

Bree was studying me like a lab specimen.

"Uh . . . haven't you heard?" I said. "Rubber bands are the latest fashion trend. My cousin just returned from Italy and said that everyone in Europe was wearing them. Very, very chic."

I covered my wrist with the other hand and stared toward the front of the bus. It was astounding what a skillful liar I had become now that I was on the road to moral thinking.

I learned one thing very quickly by wearing a rubber band: I had deviant thoughts a lot more often than I realized. About every thirty seconds. Of course Mr. Bowman's class was a danger area. The hallway between classes was a minefield too. But even biology with Mrs. Tate wasn't safe. During a movie on the Great Barrier Reef, when we were supposed to be taking notes on the sea life, my mind kept straying to the tanned Australian marine biologist who ran a rehabilitation program for injured sea turtles. Did other guys think about women as much as I thought about men?

By the end of the day my wrist was as swollen as if it had been attacked by an army of angry wasps. When I boarded the bus to go home, I shielded my eyes so as not to see anyone or anything that might trigger another wayward thought. I did catch a glimpse of Bree talking on her cell phone. Prominently displayed on her right wrist was a mauve rubber band.

· ■ · ■ · ■ · ■

"Hey, you! Have you bought your Beaver Lake Booster Band yet?"

Bradley Lenihan, student council secretary, confronted me the moment I walked into school. He was stationed at a long table just inside the front doors. Bree Caruthers was behind him, taping a large colorful poster to the wall:

BEAVER LAKE BOOSTER BANDS! $2 EACH!

"Everyone in Europe is wearing them," Bradley informed me, shaking a large wicker basket filled with rubber bands. "It's the latest fashion trend in Italy. Very, very chic."

"Already got one," I said, holding up my wrist. Today's rubber band was on my left wrist. If I alternated right wrist/left wrist, maybe I could delay the onset of gangrene.

"That's not an official Beaver Lake Band," said Bradley. He shook the basket with more force. To my untrained eye, the bands in his basket looked exactly the same as the one I was wearing.

"If you don't want one for yourself, then buy one for your girlfriend. They're guaranteed to drive the ladies wild."

What choice did I have? I bought three.

The rubber band craze went ballistic the following week. The cheerleaders sold strawberry-scented rubber bands between classes. The school's Teens for Christ sold rubber bands at lunch with the initials wwjd? printed on them. The one guy at school who called himself the Atheist League sold black rubber bands on which he had tried to write "Religion is the Opiate of the Masses," although it was kind of hard to read any of the lettering.

It wasn't rare to see kids with a rainbow of fifteen or twenty rubber bands running up and down the length of both arms. You'd think their fingers would have fallen off from the lack of circulation. Other kids showed their solidarity to a particular group by wearing multiple bands of the same color; the more orange and black bands you wore, the bigger basketball fan you were.

Too bad I hadn't thought to buy stock in rubber. I could have retired wealthy by the time I got my diploma.

"Not on your life," said Rachel. "I'd rather feed my money to a cat."

Rachel and I were eating lunch together in the cafeteria. A couple of juniors had approached our table and tried to sell her rubber bands that read, STRETCH YOUR MIND — JOIN THE CHESS CLUB.

"What's wrong with showing school spirit?" I asked. With the number of rubber bands flooding the school, the single one on my wrist didn't attract any attention.

Rachel shook her head. Today's hair was brilliant orange and clashed fiercely with her purple peace symbol earrings.

"It has nothing to do with school spirit, Steven. It's all an attempt to cash in on conformity. Join the herd and buy a band. It's capitalism at its ugly worst."

Even though I didn't always agree with her opinions, I was glad to be eating with Rachel again. I had forgotten how nice it was to sit with someone who actually included me in her conversation.

"Who do you think dreams up these ideas?" she asked.

"Beats me," I said, taking a sudden interest in my cup of Jell-O salad.

She offered me one of her homemade biscotti. As I took it, she looked at the band on my wrist.

"Frankly, Steven, I'm surprised. I've always thought you had more sense than to fall for these stupid fads."

▪ ▪ ▪ ▪ ▪ ▪ ▪ ▪

Not only was I the reason for our school's rubber band mania, I was also the reason for its demise.

It was during health class, and we were discussing the chief sources of stress in a teenager's life.

"Parents."

"School."

"The uncertain future of our ailing planet."

This last response came from Rachel.

As kids called out answers, Mr. Bowman listed them on the board. Today he was wearing a pair of navy blue chinos that tightly hugged his narrow hips.

Time for another snap.

I gave a pull and the rubber band broke. Frustrating, yes, but by now I had learned to carry a pocketful of spares. This time, however, when the band broke, it went sailing across the room and nailed Mr. Bowman in the exact spot where I had been looking.

Mr. Bowman stopped writing and placed his hand on his back pants pocket. Then he turned around and faced the class.

Did Mr. Bowman know it was me? Was I about to face detention? Expulsion? Exile to another homeroom?

He picked up the rubber band and examined it. Was he looking for fingerprints? I shoved my guilty hands beneath my desk.

When Mr. Bowman finished his inspection of the rubber band, he announced, "Good. I was afraid this might have been sold by the hockey team. I can only hope that my guys are selling merchandise of a higher quality than this."

He tossed the squiggle of rubber onto Corcoran's desk and resumed his writing.

My blood began to flow again. Disaster avoided.

Or so I thought.

The next hour was geometry with Mrs. Moe. She too was writing at the blackboard when someone pegged her with a rubber band. This time it was definitely not me.

A few of the guys in the back snickered. The rest of the class held its breath.

Mrs. Moe turned around and planted her fists firmly on her ample hips.

"Excuse me?" she said.

How could two simple words sound so deadly?

That was all it took to end both the laughter and the missile practice. Until next hour. During biology the overhead projector, the chart of the human skeleton, and the stuffed deer head above the clock all suffered multiple hits from well-aimed shots.

Then came lunch.

I was standing in the salad bar line when an orange rubber band lobbed across the cafeteria and landed in the middle of the hockey table.

"Basketball rules!" somebody hollered.

In less time than it takes to pull the pin from a hand grenade, Dwayne was firing back.

"Basketball sucks! Hockey is king!"

His rubber band landed in the applesauce on a cheerleader's tray.

After that, it was all-out war.

Kids climbed onto tables, dove behind trash barrels, made fake death leaps off of chairs. Anything that moved was fair game. It was the gunfight at the O.K. Corral reenacted right there in the cafeteria. All that was missing were a few tumbleweeds and the theme song from *High Noon*.

Rubber band sales quadrupled that afternoon. Groups of students huddled in classroom corners, diagramming their battle strategies for an even bigger operation in the lunchroom tomorrow.

Then, just before the dismissal bell rang, our vice principal, Mr. Cheever, made an unscheduled appearance on the classroom monitors. He looked even grimmer than usual.

"It has come to our attention that there has been an inordinate proliferation of rubber bands here at Beaver Lake."

He held one up to the video camera in case we didn't know what they looked like.

"While a rubber band can be a useful tool, it can also be a dangerous, life-threatening weapon. Due to recent student misuse of these objects, and in light of the many students and staff who suffer from serious latex allergies, we have been forced to institute a new zero-tolerance policy. Beginning tomorrow, anyone caught in possession of a rubber band will be subject to an immediate one-day suspension. Subsequent violations will result in police involvement. A letter to this effect is being mailed to your parents."

He dropped the offensive weapon into a wastebasket at his feet.

"We thank you for your understanding in this important issue. Have a nice afternoon."

CHAPTER
NINE

There was no longer any use denying it. I had turned into a hardened criminal. I stole from the public library. I had assaulted my favorite teacher. I had lied to my fellow classmates, including my best friend. And now, every day beneath the cuffs of my sweaters, I was smuggling illegal and dangerous weaponry into the school.

Might as well sign me up now for a guest spot on *America's Most Wanted*.

■ ■ ■ ■ ■ ■ ■ ■

"Steven is such a good son," said my mother.

She was sitting in our immaculate living room with a reporter from the *Beaver Lake Beacon*, being interviewed about her *Clean Teen* book.

"He's a wonderful example of how a young person can learn to be just as tidy as any adult."

Fifteen minutes earlier I had been rushing from room to room, cleaning as fast as possible. "If you can't find a place for it, just throw it down the basement," called my mother as she shoved dirty dishes into the oven while applying lipstick in the microwave's reflection. We had finished our cleaning blitz only seconds before the reporter arrived at the door.

"Refreshments?" I asked the young woman, holding out a tray of instant coffee and a platter of cookies.

She stopped taking notes and helped herself to an Oreo.

"Not only neat, but polite," she told my mother. "Some girl is going to get herself a terrific husband."

"She certainly is," said my mom.

* * *

I was naked, standing in the middle of an ice arena. The Beaver Lake hockey team was surrounding me while my family and friends watched from the stands.

"At the count of three, fire!"

An unseen female voice with a heavy Norwegian accent led the count.

When she reached "three," the hockey players pulled off their gloves and began riddling my body with rubber bands. I couldn't move, not even to cover myself.

Suddenly two strong arms embraced me from behind. I was lifted off my feet and into the air. The ice rink and the hockey players and everyone in the stands disappeared as I was carried through the sky to a secluded hill. Once on the ground, my rescuer wrapped me in his warm red cape. When I turned to thank him, I discovered that it wasn't Superman who had saved me. It was Mr. Bowman.

"Steven! Wake up!"

I didn't want to open my eyes. Once I did, I knew that the safe, comforting sensation of Mr. Bowman's arms around my chest would vanish. I knew I would no longer be on that secluded hill. I also knew I'd have to snap myself with a blasted rubber band.

"Steven! You're going to be late!"

I dragged myself out of bed and stumbled to my desk. I lifted the lid from the antique Superman cookie tin where I stored my school supplies and slipped a fresh rubber band over my wrist. Halfheartedly, I pulled it back.

Snap.

▪ ▪ ▪ ▪ ▪ ▪ ▪

My mom was right. I was late for school.

I might have made it to homeroom on time, but Evan Jenkins and Sue Mason, captains of the boys' and girls' basketball teams, were making out in front of my locker. It took them forever to untangle their long arms and legs and move. Add to that the obstacle course of hand-holding couples in the hallway, so that by the time I slid into my seat, I was more than a minute late.

I hated being late for homeroom.

"Glad you could make it, Steven."

The friendly warmth of Mr. Bowman's voice made all of my rushing worthwhile. For an instant, I was on that secluded hill again.

Rats.

I reached inside the cuff of my sweater, looped a finger beneath the rubber band, and . . .

. . . changed my mind.

No. I wasn't going to do that to myself anymore.

Instead, I opened my notebook and wrote:

TRENT BEACHUM IS A BIG FAT IDIOT.

All the weeks of aversion therapy had not changed any of my feelings. Except for one. I had learned to hate rubber bands. From now on, I was a confirmed paper clip user.

Once and for all, I was through with Trent. If I truly wanted to make sure that I wasn't gay, there was only one thing left for me to do, and the answer had been all around me. In the halls, in the cafeteria, in the backseat of the school bus. Why hadn't I noticed it sooner?

I needed to start dating.

Everywhere I looked there were couples. Wasn't it about time that I joined them? After all, how could I know what I was missing unless I gave it a try?

Armed with my yearbook and a sheet of paper, I began my quest for a suitable dating partner that very afternoon. Flipping through the pages, I jotted down the names of potential candidates. A lot of girls had to be eliminated because they were already dating somebody else, but that still left plenty to consider. The decision wasn't going to be easy.

Then I spotted her. A good conversationalist. A thoughtful and considerate person. We even shared a mutual interest in trendy worldwide fashion accessories.

Bree Caruthers. The perfect date.

How could I possibly be gay if I was dating the most popular girl at school?

I found Bree's private listing in the phone book and got ready to dial. Sure, this was a long shot, but why not aim high? So what if she said no? So what if she laughed hysterically? So what if she told everyone at school that I was a nutcase for even considering she might go out on a date with me?

I punched her number quickly before I convinced myself that I didn't stand a chance.

"Hello?"

With that single word Bree conveyed confidence, poise, and charm. I guess that's how she became Miss Teen Hockey Stick.

"Hi, Bree. This is Steven, from school."

Silence.

"Steven DeNarski."

Silence.

"The guy who told you about the rubber bands in Europe."

"Oh hi, Steven. Thanks for the tip. The student council raised over eight hundred dollars before Cheever spoiled everything."

"Have you considered selling paper clips?" I suggested. "I bet they'd make great necklaces, or even earrings. By the way, how would you like to go out on a date?"

No sense beating around the bush. I wasn't going to change my life by making a lot of small talk.

Silence.

I picked up the yearbook and resumed my search for an eligible soul mate.

"Sure, Steven. I'd love to go out with you."

The yearbook slid between my knees and hit the floor.

"My life coach has been on my case for months. He said I need to relax and develop some relationships based strictly on fun. Going out on a date should make him happy."

Then she lowered her voice. "Besides, I've always thought you were kind of cute."

Really? Somebody besides my mother thought I was cute?

"What did you have in mind?" she asked.

"How about a movie, next Friday?"

My ready reply made me sound like a regular dating pro.

"Sorry," she said. "I've got an orchestra concert."

"Saturday?"

"I'm taking a leadership seminar all day. In the evening I've got a volleyball game."

"Sunday?"

"Sunday is the day I volunteer at the nursing home."

"The following week?"

"Rehearsals for the school musical begin. After that, my schedule gets pretty tight."

Summer vacation? Three years after we graduate?

"Let me grab my planner, Steven, and I'll see what's available."

While Bree punched dates into her electronic planner, I glanced at the DC Comics calendar tacked above my desk. With the exception of Monday evening square dancing, my schedule was wide open.

"Good news, Steven. My kickboxing instructor just had her appendix out. I'm free Monday evening from four to seven. Then I have to be home to give the twins next door their violin lessons."

"Then Monday it is," I said. Square dancing could be put on hold for something as important as this. "I'll pick you up at four."

We hung up, and I drew a bright red star around Monday. Today was Friday. That only gave me a few days to make the necessary preparations. My first date was a once-in-a-lifetime event, and I was determined to make it perfect.

"Mom, I need my license."

My mother was standing in front of an open suitcase, surrounded by piles of unfolded laundry. She was packing for a trip to Minneapolis to read from her book at a parenting seminar.

"Have you finished your two hundred hours of behind-the-wheel?"

"Practically," I told her.

"And what does 'practically' mean?"

I double-checked my notebook.

"One hundred and eighty hours and sixteen minutes. I'm less than twenty hours short."

"Then it shouldn't take you long to finish."

She dug through a tower of blouses on her nightstand till she found the one that she wanted, then expertly pulled it out without toppling the pile.

"But I need my license before then," I said.

"And what could possibly be so important that you'd consider breaking an agreement with your own mother?"

I crossed my fingers and prayed that she wouldn't be upset by my newly expanding social life. "I'm going out on a date."

She dropped the fistful of socks and clutched her chest. I prepared myself for an onslaught of objections.

"A date? Steven! That's wonderful!"

She ran across the room and wrapped me in a smothering hug. Then she dragged me by the wrist into the living room where my dad was hidden behind a newspaper.

"Edward! Guess what? Steven's got a date!"

My dad lowered his paper, a clear indication of the magnitude of the news.

"When did this happen?" asked my mom. "What's her name? Where are you going?"

"Is she pretty?" asked my dad.

"Of course she's pretty," I answered. "She happens to be Miss Teen Hockey Stick."

My dad exchanged looks with my mother.

"That's my boy," he said.

As I filled my parents in on the specifics of my upcoming date with Bree, the two of them beamed as if I had just won the Nobel Peace Prize. All of my neatness and good grades had never made them so happy. I should have started dating years ago.

"I'm supposed to pick her up on Monday, after school. That's why I need to get my license this weekend."

A small gray cloud settled upon my mother's sunny face. "I don't know, Steven. We had a deal. Two hundred hours is two hundred hours. Couldn't you invite her over here instead? The two of you could watch television and maybe play some Scrabble."

Even my dad looked mortified at this suggestion.

"Nobody plays Scrabble on a date," I told her.

"Cut the kid some slack," added my dad.

My mother resisted. "I just don't think that he's ready for his license yet. The highway is a dangerous place for somebody his age."

"For crying out loud," said my father. "Sitting in the bathroom is a dangerous place. If the kid is ready to date, then he's ready to drive."

My mother wavered, then finally gave in.

"On one condition. Steven can take his behind-the-wheel test first thing Monday morning *if* the two of you spend the weekend practicing. Agreed?"

"Agreed," I said.

My mother sat down on the arm of my father's chair. He was already back to reading the paper.

"I'm only sorry that I won't be around to meet your young lady," she said.

"Don't worry," I told her. "You'll have plenty of chances in the future. We'll probably be dating for years."

CHAPTER TEN

BAM! BAM! BAM!

My father pounded his fist against my bedroom door.

"I'm leaving in fifteen minutes, Steven, with or without you."

I squinted at the clock on my nightstand.

4:30 A.M.

My father had been called into work on Saturday and was too tired to take me driving by the time he got home. "We'll go tomorrow," he had said. "In the morning."

In my book, 4:30 was still the middle of the night.

"Can't we wait a few hours?" I called back. Like four or five or ten?

My father opened my door. The salty smell of bacon from the skillet in his hand filled the room.

"Ice-fishing derby," he said. "Up at Round Lake. Great chance for you to practice your driving."

Ice fishing ranked right up there with leg amputation on ways I wanted to spend my weekend.

I pulled the comforter over my head and snuggled closer to my pillow.

"Five minutes!" called my dad from the kitchen.

A vision of my driver's license shook me from my sleep. Why did I have to make that promise to my mom?

I climbed out of bed and pulled on layers of clothing until I couldn't bend. Then I grabbed a cold piece of bacon from the kitchen and met my dad in the garage.

"Help me with this tarp," he told me.

Together we pulled a green sheet of plastic off my dad's pickup, a refugee from my grandfather's farm.

"Can't we take your car?" I asked.

"You don't take a car ice fishing," he said. "You take a truck."

My father's truck looked like it was ready to collapse. The windshield was cracked. The fenders were attached with coat hanger wire. The headlights were held in place with a roll and a half of duct tape.

"Toss those plastic pails in the back," he said as he patted the Ford's rusty sides. "And don't scratch the paint."

When the back was loaded with all of our gear, my dad

hauled himself into the cab. "Let's go!" he told me. "The fish are waiting!"

I took a deep breath and began a losing wrestling match with the stick shift. After killing the engine fifteen or twenty times, and after twice as many swear words from my father, I managed to get us out onto the highway.

When we had been rattling down the road for a few miles, I gave my father a quick glance to see if he was satisfied with the way I was handling his truck. His eyes were closed and his chin was bouncing up and down against his barrel chest. Hardly the close supervision that my mother had ordered.

My dad woke up several hours later when we reached the outskirts of Round Lake. After a brief stop at Randy's Bait and Beer to get us registered for the contest, he directed me to a boat ramp that led out onto the frozen lake.

I drove to the edge of the ice and stopped. An impatient Hummer behind us nearly shattered our windows with its horn.

"What's the problem?" my dad hollered over the roar of his sputtering truck.

"Is it safe?" I hollered back. In Driver's Ed we had watched several films about teenagers driving onto ice that was too thin. Their terrified faces as they plunged to an icy death were still vividly etched into my brain.

My father swept his hand across the windshield,

indicating the dozens of trucks, snowmobiles, and SUVs scattered across the lake. If they were willing to risk their lives, why not us?

I inched the truck forward and prepared to leap for safety the moment we started to sink.

We parked near a ring of ice houses. The sun was just creeping over the trees that edged the lake and the sky was a soft mixture of pink and purple and blue. Mornings would be beautiful if they didn't happen so early in the day.

While I unloaded the truck, my dad fired up his gas-powered auger. The four-foot-long drill with a nasty revolving blade could have easily been the weapon of choice for a psychopath in a horror film. He drilled two grapefruit-sized holes, then placed an upturned pail beside each.

"Have a seat," he told me.

I watched as he skewered a wiggling minnow onto his hook and dropped it into the water. He then slid the styrofoam bait bucket toward me. After spearing an innocent minnow myself, I dropped my line into the hole and our day of wintertime fun began.

For my dad's sake I attempted to show an interest in this sport, but it was difficult. Soon my mind wandered. I looked around the lake and tried to predict which vehicle was most likely to break through the ice first (a forty-foot motor home towing a trailer with two snowmobiles). I picked out my favorite ice house (one painted with palm trees — at least it gave the illusion of warmth). I slid the lid off the bait bucket and began naming the fish (Flash, Zippy, Tom).

I also thought about my date tomorrow with Bree. I pictured us driving back from the movie, my new driver's license lying prominently on the dashboard. Romantic music, like Mozart or the theme from *Titanic*, would be playing on the CD player. When we reached Bree's house I would walk her to the door. We'd smile at each other and Bree would lean toward me. Our lips would meet and before I knew it . . . whammo! I'd discover that I was attracted to girls after all.

"Thirsty?" asked my dad. He popped open a beer, then tossed me a can of soda. It was ice cold, like everything around me.

My dad pulled in his line and began changing his bait for the fiftieth time.

"Dad, did you date very much before you got married?"

He plucked another doomed minnow from the bait bucket. "Some."

"Was it fun?"

"More fun than working on your grandfather's farm."

Not the enthusiastic response I had wanted.

He dropped his line back into the water and I took a big swallow of my freezing pop. "Did you always want to date girls?"

My dad looked up from the hole.

"As opposed to dating what, Steven? Gorillas? Of course I always wanted to date girls."

I jiggled my pole a couple of times.

"I mean, when did you really start liking girls? When did you go out on your first date?"

My dad put down his beer. He looked past the ice houses; the wrinkles above his brow, which I always thought were permanent, disappeared. "Carolyn Kubitschek," he said. "She was the first. Prettiest girl I've ever seen."

He looked at me and the wrinkles reappeared. "Don't you dare tell your mother I said that, okay?"

He grinned and shook his head.

"My best friend bet me ten bucks that I didn't have the guts to ask her out. You better believe she scared the crap out of me when she said yes."

I tried to imagine my dad being scared about anything.

"I took her to a concert in St. Paul. Can't even remember the band, but I'll never forget the ride back home."

His grin grew even wider.

"How old were you?" I asked.

"A senior in high school."

A senior? Ha! I was only a sophomore! I had been worried for nothing. The DeNarski men were simply late bloomers!

"So that was the first time you ever thought about girls

romantically? Carolyn Kubitschek, when you were seventeen or eighteen?"

My excitement was causing me to shake, or else it was the windchill of twenty below.

"Hell no. There wasn't a girl in high school who didn't drive me wild. I just never had the nerve to do anything about it."

Oh.

I had only been in high school a year and a half. Maybe if I started going wild now, I could make up for lost time.

"And then there were the Peterson sisters in junior high," continued my dad. "If I wasn't drooling over them during the day, I was dreaming about them at night."

Thank goodness my dad didn't know about my junior high dreams.

"But my first big crush came in sixth grade. Miss Fox. God help me, that was her name. I swear she wore skintight sweaters just to keep us rowdy boys in line. As long as we were watching her, we were too busy to get into trouble."

Sixth grade? My father was already interested in girls by the time he was twelve? I let the end of my pole sink into the ice hole.

My dad gave my tennis shoe a kick with his boot. "Stop worrying, Steven. Everyone gets nervous about his first date. You're a DeNarski. The DeNarski men have always been a hit with the ladies."

My pole jerked suddenly and almost disappeared down the hole.

"Watch it!" he said. "You've got a bite!"

I pulled on the line until a walleye the length of my bedroom pillow slid through the opening. It flipped around on the ice as my dad tried to catch it with his hands.

"Impossible," he said, after taking the hook from its mouth. "You've been using the same dead minnow all day."

I guess some fish like their dinner well-aged.

My father helped me register my catch at the weigh-in tent. Six pounds, two ounces. We then stood around drinking hot chocolate from a concession stand until it was time for the winners to be posted.

I was on my fourth cup of cocoa when a tall, skinny man in a fluorescent hunting cap began announcing the weights of the top fish. He started with twentieth place and worked his way up. When he got to the top five, my fish was still a pound heavier than anything else.

Fifth place, fourth place, third place were announced. Second place went to a six-pounder.

"You did it!" said my dad, slapping me on the back. "You won!"

When my name and winning fish were called, my father

pushed me forward so I could claim my prize. The crowd applauded and whistled as the announcer helped me up onto a tiny makeshift stage. A photographer from the local paper almost blinded me with all the pictures he took.

"What did I win?" I asked. The second-place fish had earned a year of free video rentals. First place had to be even better.

The announcer pointed with his mittened fingers. All eyes turned to a glistening, midnight black, monster pickup truck that had been backed into the tent.

My jaw dropped open like a dying walleye.

A pickup! A brand-new pickup! I momentarily forgot that I was a mature sixteen-year-old on the brink of adulthood and leaped into the air and screamed. What perfect timing! Bree would go crazy when I pulled up to her house in this. I'd be an instant celebrity at school. Maybe even Mr. Bowman would ask for a ride.

"You have won a brand-new collapsible fish house!"

The announcer pointed to the back of the truck. A big box labeled FISH IGLOO III rested on the pickup's bed. The graphics on the box showed a gleeful fisherman stepping out of a tentlike structure in the middle of a frozen lake.

The crowd of onlookers *oohed* and *aahed* like the audience on a game show when a self-cleaning oven was unveiled.

"What have you got to say to that, young man?"

He pushed a microphone close to my mouth. The throng of envious anglers wrapped in their scarves and parkas waited for my response.

I looked at the ice house, then back at the crowd. My dad was standing proud in the front row.

"I've never been happier in my life," I said.

By the time we got my prize loaded onto our truck, it was dark. My dad fell asleep the moment we hit the highway.

Okay. So maybe I didn't win a pickup. Tomorrow I was going to get something even better.

I slapped my cheeks to keep from falling asleep.

Tomorrow I was going to get my license, a girlfriend, and a life-changing date.

CHAPTER
ELEVEN

y dad and I were at the driver's exam office a half hour before it opened.

"You're in luck," said the clerk at the license counter. "Our first appointment canceled. We can fit you in right away."

Everything was working out perfectly.

My examiner was a short, round man with a fluffy white beard that reached his waist. "Call me Sam," he said, shaking my hand. His eyes were bright and his cheeks were pink. He looked as much like Santa as the man they hired each Christmas at the strip mall. Then I realized that he *was* the man they hired.

As Santa struggled to make the seat belt reach across his lap, I reviewed the parting advice my dad had given me:

"Drive like you're afraid, Steven, and that examiner will think you're a coward. Drive with confidence, and you'll earn his respect."

"You can start the car when you're ready," said Sam.

With a strong, sharp twist, I cranked the ignition, hoping Sam noticed the confidence in my wrist.

He instructed me to pull out onto the street. I did so, swiftly and boldly. Sam nearly rolled over on top of me. "Whoa, take it easy!" he exclaimed, rolling back to an upright position.

Okay, maybe that was a little *too* confident. I checked my speed, then proceeded down the street.

It had started to snow. Not little sugary flakes, but thick, wet, sticky flakes that splattered against the windshield. I turned on the wiper blades, but they only smeared the snow around into a blurry film.

"Go ahead and take a right at this next corner."

I squinted through the windshield. Did Sam mean this first corner coming up, or the *next* corner after it?

My confidence began to slip.

I didn't want to sound stupid by asking which corner he meant, but then again, I didn't want to turn at the wrong place either.

The snow was coming down harder now, like fat gray moths attacking the car.

Best just to make a decision. Be confident, my dad would

tell me. Be decisive. Show this guy you know how to handle a car. I chose the second corner and prepared to turn.

That's when I noticed the stop sign.

I hit the brakes hard, but the car didn't stop. Instead, we glided into the intersection, spinning like those amusement-park rides where you twist the wheel in your cart until you get sick and throw up. Street signs, streetlights, three-story office buildings sailed past as we spun in a circle. When we finally stopped, we were pointed in the direction that Sam had asked me to turn.

Sam didn't say anything. Neither did I. Maybe, just maybe, he hadn't noticed. It was my only hope.

I proceeded forward.

"Take another right turn," said Sam.

This time my stopping and turning were models of perfection.

"And another."

Exquisite execution.

"And one more right."

Professional to the extreme. I could have starred in an instructional movie on perfect right turns. Surely I must have proven that I was a master at turning. Surely Sam could see that.

"And pull up to the curb."

We were back in front of the exam building.

"That's it," said Sam. "You failed."

Failure was not on my schedule for the day.

"You went through a stop sign," he continued. "Automatic failure."

He unfastened his seat belt and pushed open his door. I grabbed his arm so he couldn't get out. "But I can't fail!" I told him. "I've got a date!"

The Santa Claus twinkle was gone from his eyes.

"Sorry, son," he said. "I hope she lives within walking distance."

■ ■ ■ ■ ■ ■ ■ ■

"Fathead city employee!"

My dad was driving me to school.

"What does he know? I've gone through plenty of stop signs in my life, and does that make me a bad driver?"

I didn't answer. I was too busy trying to think of a way to rescue my date with Bree.

"The world is full of jerks, Steven. Don't let the idiots stop you from getting what you want." He pounded on the steering wheel for emphasis. "We'll come back next week and show that moron that you can drive circles around anyone on the road."

I had already shown Sam that I could drive circles. I needed to show him that I could stop at stop signs.

We arrived in front of the school.

"Dad, about my date today . . ."

It wasn't the ideal solution, but it would have to do.

". . . could you drive us to the movies?"

"Can't," he said. "I'm working late."

My plans were falling apart faster than I could rewrite them.

"But Dad, you don't understand!"

My voice was louder than either of us expected.

"Calm down, Steven. It's not the end of the world. Take the girl out next week."

She wasn't available next week. Or next month, for that matter. Maybe not even next year. If I wanted a date with Bree, it had to be today.

⠀⠀⠀⠀⠀⠀⠀⠀

It was only when we were boarding the bus to go home that I finally managed to locate Bree. I helped hoist her backpack up the steps.

"Thanks, Steven," she said. "I'm really looking forward to this evening."

"Me too," I said. "But first, I'm sorry."

"For what?"

She and her backpack took a seat. I sat down behind her.

"I've been incredibly chauvinistic. It was wrong for me to assume that I'd be the one driving. Maybe you want to drive. Plenty of people find driving therapeutic and restful."

She smiled her beauty-queen smile. "You are such a thoughtful guy," she said. "I'd love to drive."

Yes!

"But I don't have a car and my mom doesn't get home till six."

She pulled a stack of tiny flash cards from her backpack and handed them to me. They were covered with strange abbreviations. "I'm taking an online chemistry class. Would you mind helping me with my inorganic compounds?"

I shuffled the deck and held up the cards, one by one. "Come to think of it," I said, "I didn't even ask if you liked movies. If you want, we could meet at the park and go skating."

"Calcium oxide. Sulfur dioxide."

"Or sledding."

"Sulfuric acid. Carbonic acid."

"Or maybe we could just go for a walk. Who doesn't like walking in freshly fallen snow?"

"Sodium hydroxide. Hydrochloric acid."

She rattled off the words faster than I could flash the cards.

"Steven, is there a problem with going to the movies?"

Bree had blazed through the entire deck of thirty cards without a single mistake. Not only was she a beauty queen, she was a scientific genius. How could I admit to a talent like Bree that I couldn't even pass a simple driving test?

"No, there's no problem. It's just that going to the movies seems so ordinary. This is our first date and I want it to be special. Memorable. Hey, I know! Why don't you come over to my house and we can play Scrabble?"

She combed her auburn hair with her long, slender fingers. Each of her nails was perfectly manicured. "That's real sweet, Steven, but a movie sounds better."

"Terrific! Then that's what we'll do."

We had reached Bree's corner.

"See you at four," she said, shouldering her pack.

"I'll be there," I replied.

It was snowing again. At least if it had been summer, Bree and I could have ridden our bikes.

I stared out the kitchen window and watched the snow cover the barbecue grill in the backyard. It wasn't fair. If I was capable of driving my dad's pickup all the way to Round Lake, didn't that prove I was a responsible driver? Why shouldn't I be allowed to drive the few miles to the movie theater?

The clock in the hallway chimed quarter to four.

Wasn't my future happiness more important than the whims of an overly critical driving examiner?

The answer was obvious: Of course it was.

My dad's pickup rattled into Bree's driveway and lurched to a stop. I turned off the engine and walked to her door.

"Sorry I'm a few minutes late," I said. "I ran into some unexpected delays."

"No problem," she said. "It gave me time to reprogram my cell phone."

I escorted her to the pickup and pulled open the rusty passenger door.

"Howdy," said a voice from inside.

"And this is my dentist, Dr. Newel."

Dr. Newel was the only adult in our family's address book who had been available at such short notice. He was a Superman collector like I was, and for months had been asking to buy my 1967 Superman lunch box (complete with original thermos). When I'd called and told him I was willing to sell, *if* he rode with me on this date, he had canceled a late-afternoon root canal and was at my house in five minutes. When he'd pulled up in his red Porsche, I was thrilled. Dr. Newel, however, insisted it was strictly a two-person car. That's why we ended up with my dad's truck, a junk heap on wheels with room for three.

"I know it's kind of weird bringing your dentist along on a date, but I—"

"You're Steven's dentist? That's fantastic!" Bree extended her hand and Dr. Newel pulled her into the cab. "I've been thinking about a career in oral surgery. You don't happen to have any good recommendations for undergraduate schools, do you?"

Dr. Newel exposed a grin full of oversized teeth. "You bet

I do!" he said. "All five of my daughters have dental practices themselves. Nothing makes me happier than guiding a young person into the rewarding field of mouth care."

By the time we got to the movie theater Dr. Newel and Bree were already arranging a summer internship program. From the enthusiastic intensity of their discussion, I was afraid I wasn't going to be able to separate them.

"Here's an idea," I said. "Why don't you write up a list of dental scholarships, Dr. Newel, while Bree and I are watching the show. By ourselves."

"Excellent thinking," he told me, taking a ballpoint pen shaped like a toothbrush from inside his coat. "I'll be waiting for you in the lobby when the movie lets out."

My time alone with Bree was dwindling. I needed to make every second count. At the ticket window I bought two admissions to the most romantic-sounding show playing, *You and Me and Love*. Then I steered Bree toward the refreshment counter. I was going to spare no expense to make this a first-class event. "Order anything you like," I said gallantly. "Cost is no —"

I stopped midsentence. A life-size cardboard cutout of Bree was staring back at me from the other side of the counter. She was dressed in a gown and a rhinestone tiara. In one hand she held a hockey stick; in the other, a tray of snacks. A sign above the cutout read,

"A modeling contract came with the title of Miss Hockey Stick," explained Bree.

We ordered two Bree Caruthers Specials. I paid while Bree signed autographs for the concession workers.

By the time we entered the theater, the movie had already begun. Bree pointed to a pair of seats in the center. An elderly couple in the same row spotted us and waved. At first I thought they were more of Bree's fans, then I realized they were waving at *me*. It was Morris and Mavis Swenson from the Busy Bees, dressed in their dancing clothes, catching an early show before tonight's dance.

"Friends of yours?" asked Bree.

I hesitated. Bree already knew that I drove a pickup with holes in the floor. She knew that I brought my dentist along on dates. She did not need to know that I was a square dancer as well. "Missionaries from church," I whispered. "Let's sit down front. I don't want to miss a thing."

We settled into our front-row seats and stowed our trays at our feet. I helped Bree off with her coat, then ever so casually draped my arm around the back of Bree's chair, allowing my hand to rest lightly on her shoulder. I had watched enough couples on television to know that this was the proper position for a boy and a girl.

Yes. This was the way the date was supposed be. Me and Bree alone, enjoying a romantic film. I leaned back and stared up at the giant screen, savoring the perfection of the moment.

The movie seemed to be about a couple of brothers, or best friends, who traveled around together. I think they were looking for girls. To be honest, I didn't give it a lot of thought. Instead, I thought about all the people in the lobby who had seen me out on a date with the most popular girl at school. If each of those people told four other people, and those four people told four more, by Tuesday morning all of Beaver Lake would know how much I enjoyed dating women.

Then I began to wonder how long it was going to take before my close proximity to Bree triggered some sort of physical interest. To be fair, it had only been a few minutes. I had the rest of the date to develop an interest in girls.

But mostly I thought about how much my arm hurt. On television, the boy with his arm wrapped around the girl's shoulder always looked comfortable and relaxed. Then why was my arm beginning to cramp, and why did my shoulder socket feel like someone was driving a nail into it? But I didn't move. I wasn't about to break the intimate mood of our date.

I turned my attention back to the film. Maybe that would distract me from the pain in my arm.

The two best friends were lying on a beach. I guess they still hadn't found any girls yet. Turquoise waves rolled onto the shore. A tropical breeze made the distant palm trees dance. I wondered when the romantic part of this movie was going to kick in.

Just then, one of the guys (the one with muscular arms and very short swim trunks) laid his head on the other guy's lap (the guy with emerald eyes and a black goatee). They smiled at each other and interlocked fingers.

The pain in my shoulder vanished.

The guy with the goatee bent closer toward his friend and they stared deeply into each other's eyes.

I leaned toward the screen.

Their lips got closer and closer, until at last . . .

I melted into the cushions of my seat as the two young men towering above me engaged in a long and passionate kiss.

"Ewwwww!"

The noise from behind us snapped me to attention. The guy on my right gagged, and somewhere a row of high school girls giggled.

I tightened my grip on Bree's shoulder.

What had I been thinking? How could I have forgotten the purpose of this date? I was here to have fun with a member of the opposite sex, not become dreamy over a pair of handsome actors falling in love.

Had anybody caught me watching that kiss? Was Bree slowly moving away from me? I was *never* going to see a movie again without thoroughly checking the reviews.

The movie continued, and whenever the two guys appeared together (which was pretty much all of the time), I closed my eyes tightly and willed myself not to listen. I was not going to risk being distracted by something so counterproductive to this date.

I prayed for the film to end, but we were obviously watching the longest movie in the history of modern cinema. Hours turned into days. Days turned into weeks.

An eternity later, when the credits finally appeared, Bree stood up and my arm fell limply onto her seat.

"So, what did you think?" she asked.

I shook my bloodless arm and rolled my head in a vague, noncommittal manner.

"I agree," she said. "It was pretty predictable."

I filled my mouth with popcorn and hoped that this was the end of our post-movie recap.

"I'm impressed that you picked this film, Steven. Some guys would have been freaked out by a gay love story."

"Gay?" I said. "Those guys were gay? I didn't notice. I think I dozed off for a while."

"I'm pretty sure my life coach is gay," continued Bree. "He's never been married, and he's always talking about his roommate, James."

"I'm planning on getting married before I'm twenty," I said. "Maybe even before I'm eighteen."

"And I bet my Uncle Mark is gay too. He moved out to San Francisco to be closer to his best friend, Craig."

I busied myself picking up candy wrappers and popcorn boxes at my feet. Why hadn't I chosen a horror flick, or better yet, a Disney film?

"So, Steven, do *you* know anyone who's gay?"

A hundred popcorn kernels choked the back of my throat.

"No," I said. "Absolutely, positively not."

The theater had pretty much cleared out by now, including the Swensons. I held up my wristwatch to Bree.

"Boy! Look at the time! We don't want to keep Dr. Newel waiting. And you've got those important violin lessons to teach."

Bree and Dr. Newel picked up their dental conversation right where they had left off. They continued all the way to her house. As we pulled into the driveway, the two exchanged phone numbers.

"Thanks for the date, Steven," said Bree as I walked her to the door. "The popcorn was stale, but your dentist seemed real nice."

We stood under her porch light looking at each other. It was my last chance to salvage this date. In fact, it was the most important moment of the evening. I knew what I was supposed to do next, I just didn't know how to begin.

Luckily, Bree did.

"You can kiss me if you want," she said.

"Of course," I told her. "That's exactly what I want."

I took a few steps closer and closed my eyes. This was where everything would finally fall into place. Even if I had blown the entire date up to this point, it wouldn't matter if I could pull off this kiss.

I aimed my head in her direction and leaned foward until our lips met. I waited for that physical attraction to start.

Maybe I was supposed to press harder.

Or maybe I was supposed to pucker more.

Or maybe I was supposed to rub my lips back and forth. The guys in the movie had definitely moved their heads back and forth during their long, intimate kiss.

I pressed and puckered and rubbed my lips against Bree's. She must have used extra-glossy lipstick, because her mouth was wet and slippery. Her lips had the feel of canned peaches. I don't like canned peaches. Not even a little.

Eventually Bree pulled back.

"Wow," I said. "That was great."

Bree wrinkled her face. "Sure, Steven. If you say so."

"You bet," I said. "Best kiss of my life."

The twins from next door came running up the sidewalk, banging each other with their violin cases. Bree followed them inside.

"See you on the bus," I called before she shut the door.

When I returned to the car, Dr. Newel grinned at me slyly. I grinned back, one man to another.

"Nice girl," he said.

"The best," I replied.

I began to whistle, just to show how happy I was.

When we arrived at my house, Dr. Newel got into his Porsche and drove off with my lunch box. I waved good-bye and watched them both disappear. It was only after I went inside and discovered that our house was empty that I figured it was safe to stop whistling. Then, very discreetly, I wiped my mouth on the sleeve of my jacket.

CHAPTER TWELVE

It was a joyless night at our house.

My mom, when she arrived home from Minneapolis, was furious because I did not get permission to go driving with our dentist. She grounded me for two weeks. My dad, when he arrived home from his overtime at the hockey stick plant, was furious because I had forgotten to put the tarp back on his pickup. He grounded me for an additional two weeks.

And I was depressed to the bottom of my soul because my date with Bree had been such a complete and total disaster.

What had I done wrong? Why hadn't our kiss made me feel good?

Had I pressed too hard?

Had we stopped too soon?

Was I turned off by the smell of buttered popcorn on her breath?

I lay in bed and worried about the reasons for my failure. Finally, at two in the morning, it dawned on me. There was only one good reason why my date with Bree had left me so unfulfilled.

She was too perfect.

How could I expect to relax and enjoy myself around someone so stunningly perfect as Bree? What I needed was a girlfriend who was as ordinary as I was. A girlfriend who didn't have a movie theater snack combination named after her.

The more I thought about this, the more it made sense. Find a girl who was not a celebrity and the pleasures of dating were bound to reveal themselves.

Relief, like a comfortable blanket, settled around me. Soon I was asleep, dreaming of attending a *Superman* film festival with Mr. Bowman.

And so I entered a period of intensive dating, a quest for my ideal mate. At first, while I was still under house arrest, my dates were limited to inviting girls home after school. We'd study together, watch a video, and yes, sometimes even play Scrabble. Scrabble is a lot more romantic than you might think. With the right tiles, you can spell some pretty intimate words.

My mother was thrilled with this arrangement. It allowed

her to meet all of my dates. In the evening, as she described to my father the merits of my date-of-the-day, she always ended with this proclamation: "I have never in my life met a nicer young lady." Until the next day, when she declared my new date to be even nicer.

By the time I had served my four-week sentence, I had racked up a total of twenty-three dates with twenty-one different girls. What other guy at school could claim such an impressive record? In fact, I was developing such a strong reputation as a ladies' man, girls were beginning to call *me* and ask for dates. Sometimes I went to their houses and helped them clean their basements, sometimes I helped them shovel their walks, and sometimes we just sat in the library after school while I listened to them confide their problems in me.

This was all well and good, except . . .

Except I still hadn't found what I was looking for. The girls were nice enough, but I still hadn't found one who triggered a single passionate emotion. Discouraged and increasingly worried, I wondered how much longer I would have to search.

But perseverance pays off. The date that would alter my life eventually arrived, and it came from an unexpected direction.

"Hello? Is this Steven? It is me, Solveig Amundson."

At first I thought our school's foreign exchange student

was calling to sell me tickets to the Norwegian Club's lute-fisk dinner and slide show.

"I am calling to ask if you would go to a movie with me."

Solveig had completely slipped under my dating radar. I had assumed she was still preoccupied with members of the hockey team.

"Sure, Solveig. A movie sounds great."

Maybe I was more compatible with Norwegians. According to our family tree, my great-grandmother's second husband had been an officer in the Norwegian National Army.

She picked me up on Sunday afternoon for an early matinee. I had spent the morning reading up on every movie currently showing in the state. There was no way I was going to be caught off-guard this time.

"Hello to you, Steven," she said as I opened the passenger door to her host family's station wagon.

A wave of dry heat rolled over me. I knew that Scandinavians were big on saunas, but I didn't expect to find one in the car.

Solveig wasn't even wearing a coat, just a silky, short-sleeved blouse and a pair of white tennis shorts. Her hair, which was usually in long braids, fluttered loosely behind her, blown by the car's heater. I unzipped my jacket and aimed the air vents away from my face, and the two of us were on our way.

Solveig proved very easy to talk with. She told me about her school in Oslo, her overprotective parents, and her eccentric grandmother who raised guinea pigs in the family's bathtub. I told her about my own family and revealed that I was a serious collector of Superman artifacts.

"I like Superman very much," said Solveig.

This date was getting better by the minute.

We were laughing and getting along so well that I didn't realize we had passed the exit for the theater until it was several miles behind us.

"Do not worry," said Solveig. "I have been shown a special way to go."

Solveig's special way was mighty long. It snaked down a single-lane road through a forest of birch and pine. It might not have been faster, but at least it was scenic.

Suddenly the station wagon stopped. The road had ended and we were sitting at the edge of a small clearing.

Solveig turned off the engine and gave me a shy look. "Here is the special way," she said.

No theater. No highway. Nobody else for miles.

She unbuckled her seat belt. A fistful of melting snow from an overhead branch landed with a plop on the hood of her car and scared me half to death.

"If you don't want to go to a movie, we could always go bowling," I suggested. "Bowling is very American."

Solveig's hand began inching across the seat. Even without the heater, the car was stifling. I tried to get some fresh air, but with the engine off, the power windows wouldn't work.

"I do not want to go bowling," said Solveig.

"Or else we could go back to my house and I could set up our foosball table. Do you have foosball in Norway?"

Solveig laughed. "You are a funny boy."

Her hand was now only a finger's length away from my leg. "I think you are a nice boy too," she added.

"Thanks," I said. "It's nice of you to say I'm nice."

"And I think you are . . ." She bit her lip as she tried to recall the right word. Her fingertips were now resting on the edge of my pants.

"Cheerful?" I offered. "A good listener? Far too polite to ever take advantage of a girl on our first date?"

She shook her head no. And then the word came to her.

"Sexy!"

I shifted my weight and accidentally hit the buckle of my seat belt. It retracted into the wall with a snap.

"And if you want," she continued, "maybe we could, how you say . . ."

She tilted her head and waited for me to fill in the blank.

Boy. Wasn't I the lucky guy. Here I was, a young man in a secluded wood with a pretty girl who obviously wanted to know me better. I should be thrilled. Ecstatic. Leaping about the car with joy.

Solveig patiently waited for my answer. I knew what that answer should be. "Yes," I said. "Let's."

She was on my lap in an instant. Her warm, moist kisses covered my face. Her long, blond hair engulfed me like a soft curtain. And her hands, they were everywhere, from the back of my head to the tops of my thighs, and every place else in between.

I swear I did my best to respond. I rubbed my hands up and down Solveig's silky blouse. I squeezed her close to my chest. I opened my mouth and allowed our tongues to tickle each other.

Solveig hummed in pleasure as her mouth moved from my lips to my ear to my neck. I echoed her hum and moved my hands to all the places they belonged. I moaned and whispered and concentrated as hard as I could. Then I fought my way through her tangled hair, gasped for breath, and shouted, "No! I don't want to do this!"

Solveig brushed the hair away from her face. "What is wrong?"

"I can't!" I said. "I absolutely, positively can't."

Solveig looked puzzled. "Why not?"

It was an excellent question. I just needed an excellent answer.

"I can't because I'm coming down with the flu."

Solveig's smile returned. "That is not a reason to worry. My doctor gave me a flu shot before I came to America!" She snuggled up close again and began nibbling my ear.

I backed into the corner by the door.

"I also think I'm getting strep throat. And a cold. And maybe even mono. It's called the kissing disease, you know."

"We do not have to kiss," said Solveig. "We could just sit and hold hands for a while. I like to hold hands." She picked up my hand and gently stroked my fingers with her thumb.

At that moment, even holding hands seemed wrong.

"Did I mention I sprained my fingers on the computer? It hurts to touch just about anything. Ouch."

Solveig looked at my fingers, then looked at my face. And then she dropped her eyes. "Oh," she said. "I see."

But I knew she didn't see at all.

She set my hand down and slid back to her side of the car. "Maybe you do not want to do anything?" she asked. "Maybe I should take you home now?"

"Maybe so," I said.

I made a pathetic attempt at sneezing, but it sounded so phony, I gave up after two *kachoos*. Neither of us said a word the entire drive back. Despite what she had told me earlier, I didn't feel funny or sexy or nice.

When she dropped me off, Solveig stared at her lap.

"Good-bye, Steven," she said. "I am sorry if what I did was bad."

No one deserved to look that sad.

Not Solveig. Not me.

I tried to think of something clever to say that would make us both feel better, but before I could think of what that might be, Solveig was gone.

"Back so soon?" asked my mom. "Where's Solveig? I wanted to tell her *god dag.* That's Norwegian for 'good afternoon.'"

"Our date was canceled," I said. "Because of the flu."

My mother set down the cup of yogurt she was eating and placed her hand on my forehead. "Then you'd better drink an extra glass of orange juice before going to bed. I don't want you getting sick too."

I climbed the stairs to my room and shut the door. Surrounding me were the hundreds of women I had carefully cut out from newspapers and magazines. They seemed to be watching, wondering what I'd do next.

I located the Victoria's Secret ad that had started my gallery. I carefully pulled it free from the wall and ripped it in two. I then did the same thing with each of the remaining photos. When the last had been removed, I carried the pieces to the garbage and returned with the phone. Then I hit the speed-dial button. "Rachel? It's Steven. Could I please come over and talk?"

CHAPTER THIRTEEN

Rachel met me at the front door with her hands on her hips. Her hair today was a stark India ink black. "It's been a while," she said.

She was right. The two of us usually spent every weekend together, listening to music, discussing our classes, writing protest letters to multinational conglomerates, but ever since dating had taken over my life, I hadn't had time for anything else. Even my lunch periods had been consumed with arranging future dates.

"I've been kind of busy," I said.

"So I've heard."

Rachel moved aside so I could enter. I carefully stepped over the golden retriever with a tail splint sleeping in the front hallway. Rachel's parents ran a veterinary clinic and their house was always filled with stray and recuperating animals.

"Could we talk in your bedroom?" I asked. This wasn't going to be a conversation I wanted her family to hear. I didn't even want the dog eavesdropping.

"Whatever," she said, and led me down the hall.

When we reached her room she scooped up a pair of gray kittens from the floor.

"Strays?" I asked.

"They were abandoned," she told me. "Someone found them in a dumpster at the laundromat. We named them Downy and Bounce."

She handed me the smaller one.

"Being abandoned really stinks," she added.

Maybe this conversation wasn't such a good idea after all.

She flopped onto her bed and put Downy on her stomach. I lowered myself onto a lime-green beanbag chair and let Bounce crawl onto my lap.

"So?" Rachel asked. "What's the emergency?"

This was it. The moment of truth.

"Rachel, I want to talk about . . ."

Bounce began to nibble on my pinkie with its tiny sharp teeth.

"The reason I've been dating so much is because . . ."

The kitten began climbing up my arm.

"You see, I've been thinking that there's a remote chance that I might be . . ."

A little sandpapery tongue began to wash the inside of my ear.

I pulled the kitten off my shoulder and set it on the floor. "Rachel, I'm . . ."

I couldn't do it. I couldn't say the words. They clung to my vocal cords, refusing to leave the safety of my throat. Once I said them, I knew I could never again pretend that they weren't true.

Rachel was sitting up now. She scooted to the edge of her bed and picked up Bounce so that both kittens were on her lap. All three of them looked at me expectantly.

I closed my eyes and booted the words out of my mouth. "I'm gay."

When I opened my eyes again, Rachel was diving toward me, arms outspread. The kittens leaped to the floor as Rachel wrapped me in a hug. "Steven! It's about time!"

She must have misheard what I said.

I tried to wriggle out from beneath her, but only slipped deeper into the beanbag. It was then, while the two of us were still tangled in a knot, that Rachel's mother walked into the room, carrying an armload of folded laundry.

"And what do we have here?" she asked.

Rachel scrambled to her feet. "Guess what? Steven finally told me that he's gay!"

"That's nice," her mother said, setting the clothes on Rachel's dresser. "Are you staying for dinner, Steven? Fred made manicotti."

Maybe I was the one with the faulty hearing.

While Rachel did a happy dance around her mother, her father appeared in the door. "Where have you been hiding, Steven? We've missed you around here. Win any more ice houses?"

Rachel's mother slipped her arm around his waist. "Steven was just telling us about being gay, Fred."

Rachel's father smiled and reached down to shake my hand. "Way to go, Steven. Just remember: safe sex, safe sex, safe sex."

The room was spinning so fast, I thought I was going to be hurled into outer space.

To complete the family picture, Rachel's ten-year-old sister, Tracy, pushed her way through the door. "Samson was on the table again, licking the silverware." Samson was the fat iguana she clutched in her arms. "Hey, why is everyone in Rachel's room?"

I finally managed to speak. "DON'T SAY IT!" I cried. "Don't you dare tell her anything!"

Immediate and total silence. Even the iguana looked

surprised. Rachel and her family waited for me to say more, but that brief vocal outburst seemed to have drained me of my vocabulary.

At last Rachel's little sister spoke. "Did Steven finally tell Rachel he was gay?"

I was going to pass out. I was sure of it.

Rachel's mother put her hands on Tracy's shoulders. "Maybe we should give Steven and Rachel some private time. Let's help your father wipe off the silverware."

She steered Tracy into the hall, and the two of us were alone again.

Rachel climbed back onto her bed and hugged her knees close to her chest. She hadn't looked this happy since her parents had installed solar panels on their roof.

I wanted to strangle her.

"I can't believe you did that," I said.

"Did what?" asked Rachel.

"Told your parents I was . . ."

I had said the word once today. Once was all I could handle.

"I didn't tell them anything, Steven. They both already knew."

This was like a very bad episode of *The Twilight Zone*. Rod Serling must be standing behind me.

"About a year ago my parents asked if I thought you were gay, and I said yes."

A year ago? Impossible! How could Rachel's family know I was gay even before I did?

I summoned the little strength I had left. "How could they tell? How could *you* tell? How could *Tracy* tell?"

Rachel sighed. "It's hard to explain."

"Try."

She twisted the friendship ring I had given her last year for Christmas. "For one thing, you've never been very interested in girls, if you know what I mean."

"What are you talking about?" I said. "The only thing I've been doing for the past month is date girls!"

Rachel didn't even blink. "Helping somebody clean out her basement is not my idea of a hot date, Steven. And neither is playing Scrabble."

Had every girl I dated given Rachel a play-by-play, post-date report? Was there nothing about my private life that was classified information?

"Okay," I said. "So what if I haven't been that interested in girls? That doesn't prove anything!" I had come to tell Rachel I was gay, and now I was trying to convince her otherwise.

"You're right," said Rachel. "It doesn't prove anything at all. What's important is who you really *are* interested in."

And for that, I didn't have a rebuttal.

"Steven, this is nothing to be embarrassed about. In

fact, it's the best news I've heard in a long time. I've been worried that you didn't trust me anymore. Now that you've told me, we're going to be closer than ever."

She stretched out on her stomach and cupped her chin in her hands. "For example, we can discuss boys together. Which guy in our class do you think is the sexiest?"

"I have no idea."

Actually, it was Victor Sanchez.

"I know," said Rachel. "Let's go through the yearbook and pick out other guys who might be gay."

There were no other gay guys at school. I was sure of that.

"Wait! I almost forgot!" She reached for the bookshelf on her headboard. "I bought this a couple of months ago so we would have plenty to talk about when you finally came out." She pulled out a magazine and spread it open on her quilt. "It's all about being gay. If you want, we can split the cost and share a subscription."

In spite of myself I leaned forward for a closer look. A lot more words than *International Male,* but maybe still of interest.

"This article is one of my favorites: 'What's Your Queer Quotient?'" She pointed to an article accompanied by a photo of sophisticated-looking young men having an in-depth discussion. "I've already read it twice, but I can ask you the questions."

Did I even have a Queer Quotient? Was this a good thing to have?

Before Rachel could start on the quiz, her mother called in through the door.

"Dinner's ready. And Fred's defrosting one of his carrot cakes so we can all celebrate Steven's big news."

Rachel closed the magazine. "You can take the quiz after we eat. Then we can look up gay celebrities on the Internet."

"No," I said. "I think I'm going to go home."

Rachel looked surprised. And then she looked worried. "Steven, are you okay?"

I didn't answer right away.

I felt shaky and exhausted, and, yes, even a little excited.

But was I okay?

"I'm not sure," I said.

Rachel slid off the bed and sat alongside me, next to the beanbag. The kittens emerged from under her dresser and began playing with my shoelaces. "That was a big step you took today," she told me. "Congratulations. You should be proud."

The muscles throughout my body relaxed a little, and I settled a bit deeper into the chair.

"And don't worry. Everything is going to be fine. I promise."

Her words sounded nice, but they were also difficult to believe.

"Are you sure you don't want to stay for dinner? My dad's carrot cake is the best. One hundred percent organic."

I shook my head no. If I stayed around much longer, Rachel's father would probably start passing out condoms.

Rachel walked me to the front door. As I pulled on my jacket, the family's golden retriever came racing around the corner and leaped at my chest. I slipped on the throw rug and ended up sitting on the floor. The dog began covering my face with wet kisses.

Rachel helped me back to my feet. "See, Steven. We all think it's great that you're gay!"

Maybe Rachel's family did, but the rest of the world was a different matter.

Then I thought of an important question.

"Rachel, you and your parents figured out I was . . ."

"Gay."

"Yeah. Well, what about my folks? Do you think that they know?"

Rachel laughed, then quickly covered her mouth. "Sorry, Steven, but I don't think your parents even know that Elton John is gay."

She was probably right about that.

We said good-bye and I started down her sidewalk, keeping an eye out for icy spots and pulling dog hair off my tongue.

So Elton John was gay, huh?

CHAPTER FOURTEEN

chool the next day was tense. Who else had figured out that I might be gay? Was that clique of freshmen girls in the hallway gossiping about me? Was that guy in biology giving me a dirty look because I had secretly noticed his sexy chin stubble? I was afraid to meet anyone's eyes for fear that GAY was scribbled in fluorescent marker all across my face.

Rachel and her family knew, but that was enough for now. More than enough. Perhaps in thirty or forty years, when both my parents were in nursing homes and I was living hundreds of miles away from Beaver Lake, I might possibly be ready to tell another person that I was gay. But until that time, being gay would be my secret identity. Clark Kent had one; so would I.

I was hoping to ask Rachel if she thought anyone else at school suspected, but she wasn't in homeroom that day. She wasn't at lunch either. She surprised me by showing up just as I was heading for the bus to go home.

"Steven! I'm glad I caught you!"

She jostled her way through the flood of students leaving the building and pulled me into the alcove where the custodian kept his snow shovels. "I promised you that everything was going to be fine, and I meant that. Here, look!"

She reached into her backpack and handed me a flaming pink sheet of paper the exact same shade as her freshly dyed hair.

Announcing the Formation of the
Beaver Lake Gay / Straight Alliance
Join other open-minded students for enlightening
discussion about this hot, hot topic!
Fun! Friendship! Healthy Refreshments!
It's time to discover why GAY is GREAT!
For more information, contact Steven or Rachel.

Our names were followed by our phone numbers.

I would have screamed, but I was afraid of attracting attention.

Before anyone else could see what I was holding, I crammed the paper deep into the bottom of my coat pocket.

"A group like this is exactly what you need, Steven. It's

the perfect place to continue your coming-out process." She withdrew a second flyer from her pack.

I grabbed that one as well and shoved it next to the first.

"I've been on the Internet all day doing research. Gay kids everywhere are starting clubs like this. It's a chance for them to open up and talk about their emotions. It's a chance for you to feel empowered."

Rachel's voice was getting louder and louder. I glanced into the hallway to make sure that nobody was listening.

"We can have guest speakers. We can discuss gay-themed books. We can even sponsor a Gay Pride Awareness Week. Plenty of schools all across the country are doing that now."

Maybe in New York. Maybe in Los Angeles. Not in Beaver Lake.

"Of course we'll have to get our club approved first, but that's just a formality. If the principal refuses, we'll take him to court. Or better yet, we'll hold a protest rally."

I saw my face splashed across the front page of the *Beaver Lake Beacon:* "GAY STUDENT AGITATOR JAILED FOR INSURRECTION."

"Nobody uses the Spanish room after school, so we can meet there, and if the club gets too big for that, we can use the auditorium."

She pulled a stack of flyers as thick as a dictionary from her pack. I grabbed them all and hugged them close to my chest, printed side against my coat.

"Your worries are over, Steven! This club is going to make you feel fantastic!" She paused for a moment to catch her breath. "So, what do you think?"

I thought I was two seconds away from having a total nervous breakdown.

"Do you want to go with me when I talk with the principal? If we catch him today, I bet we could get the club up and running by next week. Who knows, we might even get a mention on tomorrow's announcements."

I counted to ten, then spoke calmly and clearly.

"No club."

Rachel looked confused. "What do you mean?"

I thought I had been pretty direct, but I repeated the words again, this time even slower.

"But how can you not want a club?"

Did I really have to spell it out for her? "Don't you get it, Rachel? I don't want anyone else to know that I'm . . ."

My throat constricted. How could Rachel expect me to join a club like this when I still had difficulty saying the "g" word?

"But Steven, that's the beauty of this club! It's for gays *and* straights. Unless they come to the meetings, nobody will know if you're gay, straight, or whatever. I'm not gay and I'm in the club."

"I don't care," I said.

"But it will be fun."

"No!"

"But think of the boyfriend potential."

"ABSOLUTELY, POSITIVELY NOT!"

I kicked one of the snow shovels leaning against the wall and three fell over in a clattering chain reaction. Rachel opened her mouth to say something, then shut it again. For the first time in our friendship, I had left her speechless.

I handed her back the stack of flyers.

"Sorry," she said after a moment. "I didn't mean to make you angry. If you don't want a club, then we won't have one."

"Good."

She zippered the flyers back into her pack, then picked up a shovel and leaned it against the wall. "I only thought it would make you feel better."

"Well, you thought wrong."

She lowered her head and stared at the floor. Then she tugged at her lock of pink hair. "Would you mind if I started the club without you?"

I didn't even have to speak. The look that I gave her was plenty loud.

It isn't often that I win an argument with Rachel and I should have been thrilled. Instead, I was miserable.

What was wrong with me? If other gay kids across the country were happy to start clubs at their school, why wasn't I? Didn't I want to feel empowered?

I climbed onto the bus and slumped into a seat. It was only my second official day of being gay and I already felt like a failure.

▪ ▪ ▪ ▪ ▪ ▪ ▪ ▪ ▪

Thank goodness for the Bees. At least there was still one place where everything was simple.

It was Beginners' Night that evening. Five prospective Bees showed up, all of them well into their Social Security years. When it came time for the lessons, Hank paired me up with a tiny woman named Bernice.

I had once seen a picture of the oldest woman in the world, a shriveled lady from Eastern Europe wrapped in a shawl and head scarf. Bernice looked like she could have been this woman's mother. Her arched body seemed ready to snap in two if touched. She was mostly deaf, which required me to shout Hank's instructions directly into her ear. She had difficulty seeing, so I gently guided her through each move by wrapping my hands securely around her waist.

Fortunately, we had just learned CPR in health class. I was sure I'd have to use it by the end of the night.

I was wrong. When Hank played his final song, Bernice was still going strong. She raised her hands above her head and called, "More! More! More!" Then she whispered something to Mavis that made both of the women giggle like second graders.

Mavis was not one to keep a secret.

"Bernice told me that dancing with a sexy man makes her feel like she's sixty again."

My face grew warm, but I bowed toward Bernice and escorted her to her grandson, who was waiting to drive her home.

⸫ ⸫ ⸫ ⸫ ⸫ ⸫ ⸫ ⸫

"Nice job with the newcomer," said Morris. "Looks like you've got yourself a girlfriend."

We were in the coatroom putting on our jackets.

"That's just like Steven," said my mother. "Always attracting the ladies. Every day he brings home another date. Girls can't keep away from him."

"Actually, I've decided to take a break from dating." My mom might as well get used to the fact that the parade of future daughters-in-law had come to an end.

"You mean you're no longer dating that girl we saw you with at the movies?" asked Mavis.

"Nope," I said. "I am not."

"There's no special girl you're seeing on a regular basis?"

"None."

I had dated my last girl, and the decision felt good.

Mavis rubbed her wrinkled hands together. "I was hoping you'd say that. I have something I want to show you."

Morris leaned toward me and whispered, "Take my advice, Geezer. Make your getaway now, while you still have the chance."

Mavis opened her purse and pulled out a photo of a girl my age. "It's our granddaughter, Belinda. Isn't she pretty?"

The Busy Bees were always flashing pictures of their grandkids, godchildren, and pets, but this time I knew it was different.

"Yes," I said. "She's very pretty."

What else could I say?

"And she's not seeing anyone special either."

"A pretty girl like that doesn't have a boyfriend?" said my mother. "Such a shame."

"That's what I think," said Mavis.

My mother turned toward me. "Don't you think that's a shame, Steven?"

"It's a real shame," I said. "Tell her I hope she finds a boyfriend soon."

I tried to push my mother toward the door, but she refused to be pushed.

"I heard there's a big dance coming up at your school," said Mavis. "Belinda loves to dance."

"Why, so does Steven!" said my mother.

I nodded my head meaningfully toward the exit. "Isn't it time for us to go, Mom?"

"Too late," whispered Morris.

"I know you would like her a lot," continued Mavis. "She's every ounce as nice as you are. Plus, she likes to fish. I've heard that fishing is your latest hobby."

Over Mavis's shoulder I saw Mr. Bowman putting on his leather jacket and getting ready to leave. *Rescue me,* I thought. *Rescue me right now.*

"Nobody is asking you to marry the girl," said my mother. "It's just a simple dance."

Mavis moved even closer, trapping me between her and my mom. "I'd consider it a favor."

How could I not do a favor for one of the Bees? All I had to do was say yes and everyone would be happy.

Everyone except me.

Everyone except Belinda.

"I'm sorry," I said. "But no."

The disappointment on Mavis's face made me wince.

"I'd love to. I really would, except . . ."

Both Mavis and my mother waited for me to continue.

". . . except I'm going to the dance with somebody else."

A small, tactful lie. Nobody gets offended. Nobody gets hurt.

"With who?" asked my mom.

"With Kelly."

It was the first name that popped into my head.

"I thought you weren't dating anyone," said Mavis.

"I'm not," I said. "We're just good friends. But we've already agreed to go to the dance, and I can't break my promise."

"If you and Kelly aren't dating, then maybe some other evening—"

"That's enough," said Morris. He took Belinda's photo out of her hand and dropped it back into her purse. "I'll hold her here, Geezer, while you make your escape. But you'd better move fast. She's stronger than I am, and I don't know how long I can restrain her."

Mavis slapped her husband on the side and he laughed. I pulled my gloves out of my coat pocket and nudged my mother toward the door. "C'mon, Mom, it's late."

Once in the parking lot I took an extra-long time scraping the frost from our car's windows. If I took long enough, maybe my mom would forget about the school dance and my fictional companion. When every window and sideview mirror was perfectly clear, I tossed the ice scraper into the backseat and took my place on the driver's side.

"Kelly," said my mom. "I like that name. Did you know that my best friend in college was named Kelly?"

I pretended not to hear.

"You'll have to get your yearbook and show me what she looks like."

"She doesn't go to our school," I said. "She's home-schooled."

"Then I bet she's bright. Just like my friend Kelly, who was our class valedictorian. Tell me some more about your Kelly."

I described the Kelly that I knew best.

"She has long, blond hair and chestnut brown eyes. She's

very affectionate, not to mention impeccably groomed and good with kids."

She also happened to be Rachel's golden retriever.

"My friend Kelly was a blonde too!" said my mom. "What are her parents like?"

Kelly's mother was a bitch and her father was run over by a motor home when he chased a squirrel into the street, but I figured that was more information than my mother needed to know. "You're distracting me, Mom. Do you want me to run off the road and hit a tree?"

"Of course not," she said. "I'll be quiet."

And she was.

Until we pulled into our garage. "Your first high school dance. I can't wait to tell your father."

She was already out of the car and going for the door. "And I can't wait to meet your date."

CHAPTER FIFTEEN

O f course you'll need a new suit . . . and new shoes . . . and a haircut. . . ."

As the night of the dance drew closer, my mother's obsession with the event intensified.

"I loved going to dances when I was your age. Those were some of the happiest moments of my life."

Then maybe she should be the one getting the makeover and not me.

"And Edward, your son is going to need money. He's got to buy the tickets, and a corsage for his girl."

I told my mother that Kelly was not my girl, in any sense of the word, but she wasn't paying attention.

"Unless you want me to order the corsage, Steven. What color will Kelly be wearing?"

"Yellow," I said. "You might even call it golden. And no, I'll take care of ordering the flowers."

I was having a hard time finding a graceful way to get out of this dance. Contracting a lethal disease was too much to hope for, and I've never been very good at staging fake illnesses, as proven by my date with Solveig. If I claimed Kelly was sick, I was afraid Mavis would rush over and fill the vacancy with her granddaughter.

With only a few days remaining, I confided in Rachel. Ever since our disagreement on the gay/straight alliance, our conversations had been limited to neutral topics on which we both held similar views, such as nuclear disarmament and global warming. But now I needed to talk to her about something more complex: how to escape from a dance that I didn't want to attend.

We were in Rachel's basement giving her family's assortment of dogs their monthly toenail clipping. I was holding a trembling Pomeranian while Rachel wielded the clippers.

"Rachel, I'm in serious trouble. My mother thinks I'm going to the dance."

"Really? With who?"

"With Kelly."

Rachel's eyes widened to the size of small planets.

"Kelly Markovitch? All-state quarterback? Way to go, Steven! When you come out, you really come out!"

She tapped a finger lightly on my chest. "You know, I've always suspected that half the football team was gay."

"Not Kelly the football player. Kelly your dog."

Kelly, who was on the floor waiting her turn, looked up at me and thumped her tail.

For the second time that month, Rachel was speechless.

I explained to her how I had been pressured into inventing a date for this dance, then waited for her to tell me I was a spineless chicken for not telling my mother the truth.

"Steven, you're brilliant!"

Since when was it brilliant being a coward?

"Taking a dog to the dance is even better than taking a guy! It's your chance to show the world that you refuse to conform to its narrow boundaries about what it means to be a couple!"

This was way too bizarre, even for Rachel.

"I can't take a dog to the dance," I told her.

"Of course you can," said Rachel. "This is America. You can take whoever you want!"

The Pomeranian we were trimming jumped off the table and began running around my feet, yapping in agreement.

"Do you know what they call people like you, Steven?"

Mentally unstable lunatics.

"Visionaries. And it's the visionaries who make this world a better place to live."

Was it typical for a visionary to feel as if he were drowning in quicksand?

"Susan B. Anthony, Martin Luther King Jr., and Steven DeNarski."

Her eyes were actually teary with admiration. "I've never met a visionary before," she said, shaking my hand.

Kelly nuzzled my leg with her nose.

"Neither have I," I replied.

I still had one avenue of escape, but I had to wait until just the right moment. It appeared after dinner, when I was helping my mother mail autographed copies of *The Clean Teen* to major newspapers across the country. I knew I'd never catch her in a better mood than this.

"Mom, I need my license."

She finished signing her name to the title page of the book that lay open, then carefully considered my request. "No, I don't think so."

She handed me the book and reached for a new one.

After I had failed my first test, my mom had insisted on another hundred hours of practice driving before I tried again. I was still over sixty hours short, but I couldn't let that stop me.

"But I need my license for the dance."

Specifically, I needed my license so I could pick up

Kelly at Rachel's house, drive her around the block for a few hours, then drop her home again without ever showing up at school.

My mother finished the inscription and blew on the page so it would dry. "Your father and I are only too happy to drive you."

That's exactly what I was worried about.

I opened another book and slid it in front of her.

"If not for my sake, Mom, then at least let me get my license for Kelly."

She didn't even look up from her writing.

"Think about it. Out of all of those wonderful high school dances, how many times did your date arrive at your door accompanied by his parents?"

Her pen slowed just a little.

"Doesn't Kelly deserve to have those same happy memories as you? How can you rob her of one of life's richest moments?"

I looked over her shoulder. Instead of "Barbara DeNarski," she had written "Baby-pie," her nickname from before she was married. I knew I almost had her.

"Shame on you for denying Kelly so much happiness, Mom. What would your friend from college say?"

It was a low blow, but I was that desperate.

"Oh all right, Steven. You win. You can take your test again."

She finished writing her last name, then added a heart beneath her signature. "I'm not so old that I've forgotten what it's like to be young and in love."

My test was scheduled for the Friday before the dance. My mother picked me up after school, having just run the car through the car wash. A cardboard lemon swung from the rearview mirror, making the interior smell like a can of furniture polish.

"You don't want to show up at Kelly's in a filthy car. No girl wants car lint on her brand-new dress."

While I waited for the examiner, my mother reviewed her endless list of driving precautions.

"And above all, don't get too cocky. Driving examiners hate young people who are overly confident. It's the worst mistake you can make."

As my mother continued with her warnings, I watched other kids my age returning from their tests. Smiling triumphantly, they proudly showed their parents their passing scores. Was this a positive omen, or was the driving examiner's charitable streak about to run dry?

"Steven DeNarski," called the clerk. "You're next."

I looked toward the door expecting to see Santa Claus.

I saw Miss Abbergast, retired first-grade teacher and connoisseur of trashy gas station magazines.

"Hello, Steven! We meet again! That's what I love about

this job; every day I get to reconnect with my former pupils."

We walked outside to our car and she settled herself on the passenger seat, clipboard balanced on top of her pink leather purse. "I'm ready whenever you are."

Remembering my mother's safety precautions, I checked the rear- and sideview mirrors six or seven times before starting the engine.

"My, what a thorough young man," said Miss A. She made a cheerful-sounding check mark on her board.

I began to relax, sensing her charitable streak was still intact.

It was a sunny afternoon with no distracting snowflakes, hailstones, or raindrops in sight. Still, a chilly shiver of panic rippled down my back as I neared the first stop sign. I made my approach slowly and stopped a good twenty-five feet before reaching the sign. Miss Abbergast made several more happy marks on my score sheet.

The entire test continued to go well, including the dreaded parallel parking. My mother had run me through the drill so many times, I could have parked a semi between the legs of a folding chair. But I wasn't about to take any chances. As soon as the car was vaguely between the orange pylons, I stopped. Why risk knocking down one of the cones? I didn't need a perfect score; I only needed to pass.

"All right, Steven. You can drive us back."

I had completed the entire test without committing a

single major driving violation. All that was left was for me to pick up my license.

I pulled into the parking space where we had begun.

"You are such a careful, cautious driver. We don't see many young men as safety-conscious as you."

"So I passed?"

"Not by a long shot."

She ripped off my test sheet from her clipboard and handed me my score: 52 percent.

"A timid driver like you isn't ready to be on the road."

From inside her purse she produced a sheet of smiley-face stickers and stuck one to the outside of my coat. "But don't be discouraged," she told me. "I'm sure you just need a little more practice."

■ ■ ■ ■ ■ ■ ■ ■

"Things always work out for the best," said my mother. "How about if I get your father to dress up in his Sunday suit and he can pretend that he's your personal chauffeur? Maybe we can even find him a cute little driving cap to wear. I bet Kelly would love that."

I doubted whether Kelly would notice anything my father was wearing unless it smelled like hamburger or one of our neighbor's cocker spaniels.

The phone was ringing as we stepped into the house. It was Rachel wanting to know the results of my test.

"Disastrous," I said. "I'm doomed to a life of parental

transportation." I then explained my mother's plan to have my dad play chauffeur.

"Parents," said Rachel. "They can be so dense. Tell your folks you're double-dating with me. Come over to my house, and we'll go to the dance together."

I could only imagine Rachel's choice for a date. Downy? Bounce? Samson the Iguana? Still, if I had to go through with this, I'd rather not do it alone. "I'll be at your house by seven," I told her.

⁞ ⁞ ⁞ ⁞ ⁞ ⁞ ⁞ ⁞

I'm not sure who was more nervous the next night: me or my mother.

"Your first school dance is such an important milestone," she told me, tugging on my coat sleeves and flattening the lapels of my jacket.

And so is your first interspecies date.

"Edward, are you ready? It's time we drive Steven over to Rachel's."

My mother had been fine with the double-dating aspect of the night, but she was still under the impression that she was going to meet Kelly. It was time to deliver the bad news.

"Mom, I'm walking over to Rachel's. A little fresh air will help me relax."

"Good idea," she said. "I'll get my coat."

When I told her I'd rather walk by myself, she looked horrified. "But when do I get to meet Kelly?"

Not within my lifetime, if I could help it.

"I forgot to tell you something important about her," I said. "She's shy. Extremely shy."

"Too shy to meet your mother? I don't bite, you know."

Neither did Kelly, unless you took away her dog food while she was eating, but I still didn't want them to meet.

"Kelly is homeschooled, and going to this dance is a big step for her. Meeting my parents on the same night might be too much for her to handle."

"But I want to snap a few pictures to send to my college friend."

"Let the boy go," said my dad. "We'll get to meet his date when she's ready."

My mother looked so crushed that I almost changed my mind. Almost, but not quite.

"Then you'll have to tell me all about the dance the minute you get home. I won't be able to sleep until I hear every last detail."

I edged toward the door and told my parents good night.

"Don't do anything I wouldn't do," said my dad.

I promised him that I wouldn't.

My mother straightened my tie one last time.

"Make sure you tell Kelly hello." She stood in the doorway and hugged herself tight. "Oh, Steven, I am so envious. You're going to have the time of your life."

CHAPTER
SIXTEEN

Rachel was waiting in her living room when I arrived. She was wearing a slinky, strapless beige dress with a thin gold chain around her neck.

She wore just the slightest hint of lipstick, and the lock of hair on her forehead sparkled with glitter. She looked great, and I told her so.

Then Kelly made her entrance. She was freshly shampooed and her fur glowed like moonlight on a lake. Around her neck she sported a bright red collar that complemented her butterscotch-colored coat. Her tail splint was gone, and if I wasn't mistaken, someone had painted her toenails. She looked great too, and I told her so.

"Are you sure you don't want to ask one of our other dogs?" said Rachel's dad. "Like Maxwell or Butch?"

"No jokes, Dad," said Rachel. "This is a big night for Steven, and we need to be supportive."

"Sorry, Steven," he told me. "I didn't mean any offense."

Rachel's mother patted me on the back. "You're a brave man, Steven. I hope you know what you're doing."

I didn't have a clue.

I was about to ask Rachel which pet she was taking when the doorbell rang. It was Victor Sanchez, my choice for sexiest guy in our grade.

"Rachel, your date's here."

While Victor greeted her parents, I grabbed Rachel's arm and pulled her into the kitchen. "What are you doing?" I demanded. "How come I'm the only one taking a date with a tail?"

"This evening was your idea, Steven," said Rachel. "Don't worry. I'm not about to steal your thunder."

My thunder? I didn't want any thunder! I didn't even want to go to this dance!

"I only asked Victor because I wanted to be there to support *you*."

"Rachel, your date is waiting!"

We returned to the living room where Victor was standing between Rachel's parents. I caught myself admiring his thick black hair and tailored suit, then quickly looked away. He was the sharpest-looking one there, but I had enough sense to keep my mouth shut.

He walked up to Rachel and handed her a single, long-stemmed rose. I looked down at the corsage box in my hands. I opened the lid and took out one of the doggie treats I had filled it with, then handed it to Kelly. She gobbled it down, and I emptied the rest in my pocket for later.

"Hey, Steven," said Victor. "How's it going?"

I caught a whiff of aftershave, the same exact scent that Mr. Bowman used. I'd have to find a bottle of that somewhere soon.

"Is your date meeting us here, or do we need to pick her up?"

"You mean you didn't tell him?" I asked Rachel.

"I wanted it to be a surprise," she said. She ceremoniously cleared her throat and announced, "Victor, Steven's date is already here. He's taking Kelly."

Victor looked around the room, his gaze finally stopping on Rachel's mom.

"The dog," I said.

His eyes traveled from the golden retriever, to me, and back to the golden retriever again. Then he let out a low whistle. "Whatever turns your crank, man."

I was about to explain that Kelly did *not* turn my crank, but Rachel began hustling us out the door. "The dance has already started," she said. "We want to make an entrance while there's still a good crowd."

We squeezed into Victor's Volkswagen with Kelly and me filling the tiny backseat. No sooner were the doors closed when Rachel launched into another speech about how I was making an important political statement with my choice of date.

"This is history in the making," she said. "A night that will long be remembered by everyone involved."

I watched Victor's reaction in the rearview mirror. I waited for him to make a wisecrack, or at least smirk. He didn't. He nodded thoughtfully, and his only comment was, "I didn't realize I was going to be a part of history."

When we arrived at school, Rachel couldn't wait to get inside. I hung back.

"Go on ahead," I told them. "I'm going to take Kelly to the . . . ladies' room." I motioned to a clump of trees alongside the parking lot. "I'll meet you in the building."

"Are you sure?" asked Rachel. "We can wait."

Kelly had spotted the trees and was tugging on her leash.

"I'll be fine," I said. "Kelly and I will make a stronger impact if we enter by ourselves."

"Good thinking," said Rachel. She slipped her arm through Victor's. "We'll be in the gym, waiting your arrival."

While Kelly took care of her doggy duty, I thought about what lay ahead. Once I set foot inside that school, I'd be labeled a freak for the rest of my life.

The wind picked up and the tree branches overhead sighed mournfully. I tightened my suit coat against the frigid evening air.

It wasn't too late. I could still avoid public humiliation. I could claim that Kelly had run away and that I had spent the night tracking her down. All I'd have to do was hide out in the cold for a few hours. All I'd have to do was invent a few more lies.

Another vehicle pulled into the parking lot. From the shadows of the trees I watched as a mountain emerged from the car. It was Dwayne Becker, dressed in a three-piece suit made from enough material to cover an ice rink. It was the first time I had seen him in anything other than his signature sweats. He walked to the passenger side and opened the door. A girl half his size climbed out. It was Solveig Amundson, dressed in a gown that shone like a disco ball.

Before shutting Solveig's door, Dwayne took off his Marlboro cap and tossed it into the car. Then the two walked toward the school, hand in hand.

I pulled Kelly farther into the shadows.

As the couple passed, Dwayne leaned down and whispered something in Solveig's ear. They laughed. I could almost feel the aura of happiness surrounding them. They were already having the time of their lives, and they weren't even inside yet.

So Solveig had found a new date. Good. She was a nice girl. She deserved to be happy.

And then, unexpectedly, I was angry.

Make that furious.

What about me? I was a nice guy. I deserved to be happy too.

I stepped out of the shadows. "To hell with what everyone thinks!"

Kelly's ears perked up.

"I've got the suit. I've got the tickets. I've even got the date. C'mon, girl. I'm going to this dance!"

Together we stormed the school and marched to the gymnasium, ignoring the few couples lingering in the hall.

Bradley Lenihan, from the student council, was sitting on a stool outside the gym. A paper banner above his head proclaimed the theme of the dance: THE FUTURE IS OURS! "Sorry, no pets," he said.

"She's not my pet," I snapped. "She's my date." I shoved our tickets into his hand and continued inside, Kelly following closely at my heels.

Walking into the gym was like walking into the world's largest roasting pan. Every conceivable surface from the scoreboards to the drinking fountains had been wrapped in aluminum foil. I guess the decorating committee had thought we'd be doing a lot of barbecuing in the future. The sight of all those male-female couples throughout the room, reflected hundreds of times on the shiny walls of the gym, caused me to rethink my outburst of self-confidence.

On the far side of the gym I spotted Rachel talking intently with Victor. Before she could see us, I pulled Kelly behind a giant cardboard flying saucer. "We don't have to let her know we're here. Not yet."

Rachel was sure to create a scene, and I wanted a few minutes to regain my courage. I hurried Kelly to an empty table in the corner of the gym, where we sat hidden behind a bunch of Mylar balloons.

A minute passed.

Then five.

Nothing terrible happened. The band played a mix of retro-rock classics, all at a volume so loud, it was difficult to tell one song from another. Girls squealed and hugged their friends and stood in groups admiring each other's dresses. A handful of couples danced boldly in the center of the gym, oblivious to everything else, including the music. No one paid any attention to us.

"I think I can do this," I told Kelly. "I think I'm ready to find Rachel."

But before I could leave my seat, our table was darkened by a shadow roughly the size and shape of a water buffalo. It was Mr. Cheever, our vice principal. "Get that filthy animal out of here," he growled.

Kelly growled back.

"And get it out *now,* before it attacks someone."

If Kelly could tolerate Downy and Bounce climbing all over her head, I doubted whether she was going to turn vicious on anyone in this gym.

"She's actually very gentle," I said, scratching Kelly behind her ears. Her back leg started twitching and her growl was replaced with a wide, canine grin.

"Out!" said Cheever.

But it was cold outside, and windy. Besides, the cheesy futuristic decorations were beginning to grow on me.

"Couldn't we just sit behind these balloons and watch?"

Cheever's face was rapidly turning the color of tomato paste. "I am not about to let some smart-aleck kid disrupt this school event. I want that dog out, and I want it out NOW!"

His ranting had drawn a small crowd.

"Hey, look! It's a dog!"

"She's so cute!"

"What's her name?"

"Is it a boy or a girl?"

Cheever jabbed his finger firmly toward the exit.

"You're not going to make them leave?" someone asked.

"He's got the best-looking date here," said a pimply-faced guy in a shiny polyester suit, who was immediately whacked by the girl standing next to him.

Then, from the back of the crowd, I heard a familiar voice.

"Let the dog dance! Let the dog dance!"

It was Rachel, sitting on Victor's shoulders and punching the air with her clenched fist. The music had stopped and hers was the only voice in the gym.

Then another voice joined in: Victor's. Before I knew it, the walls were echoing with Rachel's demand as all of the students joined the chant.

Fifteen minutes ago I would have embraced any excuse to get out of this dance, but now . . . well, why should I allow Cheever to tell me who I could, or could not, choose for my date?

I pushed back my chair and stood up. I didn't quite reach Cheever's double chin, but I straightened my shoulders and said, "Sorry, Mr. Cheever, but we're not leaving. Our tickets said nothing about discrimination against dogs. The future is ours, and we're staying for the dance!"

The gymnasium exploded in a cheer.

Cheever glanced nervously at the mob of well-dressed teenagers poised on the brink of a riot. With one last huff, he stomped off.

After that, everyone wanted to walk Kelly around the dance floor, scratch her tummy, or bring her a glass of punch. When the band asked for requests, people shouted:

"'Who Let the Dogs Out'!"

"Something by Three Dog Night!"

"'You Ain't Nothin' but a Hound Dog'!"

I thought this last suggestion was a little tacky, but Kelly didn't seem to mind.

Even Dwayne and Solveig stopped by our table.

"You Americans are very strange," said Solveig. "But I'm glad you found a date that you like."

Dwayne just looked at Kelly and said, "I don't get it."

When it came time for the final dance, a slow one, I trotted Kelly around the dance floor myself. I smiled as I recognized the strains of "She's Always a Woman to Me."

It was then that I spotted Mr. Bowman standing behind the punch bowl, dressed in a midnight black tux. He watched Kelly and me weave our way around the other couples, then gave us his nod of approval.

Eventually the last dance ended. The band began to pack up, and the gym slowly emptied of couples.

"One more thing," Rachel said. She led all four of us into the hall where a professional photographer had his camera.

"Smile!" he said. Then he snapped a picture of us against a backdrop of moons and planets.

"You and Kelly were the stars of the night," Rachel whispered as we walked to the car.

On the way home we stopped at the Hungry Beaver Drive-Thru. Rachel and Victor ordered veggie burritos; Kelly and I shared a quarter-pound Burger Basket. While we ate, we reviewed our favorite songs of the night, critiqued the band's performance, and took turns giving our best

Cheever impersonation. Soon we were laughing so hard, we could hardly speak.

"Awesome dance," said Victor, wiping the tears of laughter from his face. He then looked in the rearview mirror and gave Kelly and me a big thumbs-up sign.

■ ■ ■ ■ ■ ■ ■ ■

"The four of us should do this again," I said.

We were making our way up the sidewalk to Rachel's front porch. I bet there were a lot of places you could take a dog on a date: the park, the zoo, the drive-in movies. I wondered if the local roller rink would make an exception to their "No Dogs" policy for an animal as well-behaved as Kelly.

I handed her the last dog treat, then opened the front door. She wagged her tail and trotted inside.

When I turned around, Victor and Rachel were still half-way down the walk.

In the glow of the porch light I watched Victor take his hands and place them gently on Rachel's waist. He took a step forward. Rachel reached up and intertwined her fingers behind his neck.

I didn't breathe.

Once, twice, they gave each other tentative pecks on the lips. Then Victor closed his eyes. Even from where I stood I could see the elegant curve of his long, dark lashes. He tilted his head low and gave Rachel a slow, graceful kiss. It was beautiful, natural, and perfect.

It reminded me of the kiss I had seen on the movie screen between the two handsome actors.

I don't know how long Victor and Rachel continued. They were still at it as I stepped around them and began the cold walk home.

CHAPTER
SEVENTEEN

"Steven? Are you up?"

I opened my eyes. Sunlight was streaming through the windows, and my alarm clock showed 11:05. Outside my door, my mother was tapping like a woodpecker. "You can't stay in bed all day!"

I knew what she wanted. Last night when I got home from the dance, I had told her I was too exhausted for a recap of the evening. She had been disappointed, but said she'd do her best to wait till the morning.

I closed my eyes and tried to make the morning go away.

"If you don't get up soon, I'll have to call Rachel and get a report from her."

"I'll be down in fifteen minutes," I said, swinging my legs over the side of the mattress.

A tell-all conversation between Rachel and my mom was not a pretty thought.

My mother went away and I sat on the edge of my bed, staring at the Superman poster on the far side of the room. It was the classic pose, hands on hips, cape billowing in the wind.

"What am I going to tell her?" I asked.

Superman stared back, dissecting me with his X-ray vision.

I turned away, but even with my eyes averted I knew what he wanted me to do. I just didn't know if I was capable of it. How could I spring the truth on a woman who thought I was dating a clone of her best friend from school?

I turned back toward the poster. Superman's expression was unchanged. Stern and resolute. But at the same time, compassionate too.

How can you win an argument with Superman?

"Okay," I said. "I'll do it. I'll tell my mother I'm gay."

・ ・ ・ ・ ・ ・ ・ ・ ・

As I stood in the shower with steamy water pummeling my scalp, I imagined my mother's reaction. Tears? Anger? Uncontrollable hysteria?

Or maybe Rachel had been wrong. Maybe my mother already knew. Maybe this revelation would come as no big deal to her.

The shower turned icy as the hot water ran out.

"Steven! I'm waiting!" called my mom from downstairs.

The time for stalling had come to an end.

＊ ＊ ＊ ＊ ＊ ＊ ＊ ＊

My mom was at the kitchen table, scissors in hand and a stack of coupons in front of her. The Sunday paper was spread in every direction.

"Finally!" she said and swept the papers to one side, making a spot for me to sit. "I'll get you something to eat while you tell me all about last night."

My stomach was flip-flopping so much I couldn't have eaten a cornflake, but I didn't bother to argue.

"There's so much I want to know. For example, who was there, who were the chaperones, did they play any waltzes. . . ."

She took a plate of last week's French toast from the fridge, briefly ran it under water, then popped it into the microwave. "But why don't you start with Kelly."

Nothing like getting to the tough subjects first.

"What did she look like? And don't spare me any of the details."

Okay, Superman, it's time to make you proud.

"Mom, Kelly is a dog."

My mother's face went blank. Then she scowled.

"Steven Killebrew DeNarski! I thought I raised you with better manners than that! How dare you refer to a young lady in that manner!"

I tried again.

"Mom, Kelly is a *real* dog."

"I don't care, Steven. That's still no way to talk about a girl."

I picked my words a little more carefully. "Mom, Kelly is not a girl. She's Rachel's golden retriever. A canine. A dog."

My mother squeezed her eyes shut and placed her fingers alongside her temples as if she were getting a headache.

"Call me old-fashioned, Steven, but why would anyone take a golden retriever to a high school dance?"

Here we go. This was it.

"Because I'm gay."

I braced myself for the hysteria.

My mother smiled. "Steven, just because you took a dog to a school dance doesn't make you gay."

"I'm not gay because I took a dog to the dance. I took a dog to the dance because I'm gay."

This explanation sounded confusing even to me.

My mother sat down at the table and folded her hands. "I love you very much, Steven. You know that, don't you?"

I nodded.

"And the only thing I want in this world is for you to be happy and safe."

This conversation was going better than I had feared.

"Therefore, you are absolutely, positively not gay."

The buzzer on the microwave went off and she went to get the French toast.

"But I am!" I said.

"No, you are not. You are much too young to be gay."

Boy, did she have that wrong. Even as I talked about last night, I was picturing Victor giving me the thumbs-up sign and seeing his dark eyes smiling at me in the rearview mirror.

She set the plate of withered French toast in front of me. "Would you like some syrup? Or maybe a little powdered sugar?"

"I'm not hungry," I said.

"Well, I'm starved." She picked up a fork and dug into the toast.

Complete dismissal was not a reaction I had expected. And as much as the topic still made me nervous, I wanted my mom to acknowledge it was real. "It's true," I said. "I'm gay."

"Mmmm!" she said. "Delicious! Can I at least get you some orange juice?"

"You're not even listening, are you?"

"Of course I'm listening, Steven." She went to the cupboard to get a glass. "You're telling me about some crazy phase that you're going through. I know all about crazy teenage phases. Believe it or not, I was a pretty wild and crazy teenager too. And if you want to pretend that you're gay for a little while, you go right ahead."

She began drinking the juice herself.

"I'm not pretending, Mom."

"You know, taking a dog to a dance is kind of cute. You've always liked animals, ever since you were a little boy. Maybe we should have gotten you a dog when you were younger. Would you like to get a dog now? I'll talk to your father. We can all go to the humane society this afternoon."

"Mom, I'm gay." I didn't know how else I could put it.

She finished the juice and started filling the sink with soapy water. Everything she could reach, she tossed into the suds. She must have forgotten that we owned a dishwasher. "Steven, I'm just too busy to talk about this right now."

She plunged her hands into the sink and pulled out a wet ketchup bottle. Even though she was hoping this conversation would go away, I needed her to hear me. "Mom, please."

"Steven. I'm sorry." She removed a clean frying pan from the shelf above the stove, dunked it in the water, and scrubbed it with the concentration of a fanatic. The sound of steel wool scraping against the aluminum pan made my teeth hurt.

Then she stopped.

She set the dishrag on the counter and looked out the window over the sink. "I need some time to think about this," she said.

I could understand that. I was still thinking about it myself.

"Would it be okay if we talk about it later?" It was both a suggestion and a plea.

"Sure," I said. Later was a compromise I could live with.

My mother's head and shoulders collapsed in relief, like a sock puppet minus its hand. Then she pulled the plug from the sink and wiped her soapy palms on her slacks. "But in the meantime, please don't mention any of this to your father. I don't think he could handle it as well as I did."

∎ ∎ ∎ ∎ ∎ ∎ ∎ ∎

It was my evening to help my dad in the kitchen. Once a week I was required to be his assistant as he made dinner. "A man's got to know how to cook," he had told me. "You never know who you might end up marrying."

His menu for the night was Exploding Chili: eight quarts of black beans, pinto beans, and kidney beans, seasoned liberally with green chilies and Tabasco sauce.

"Pepper," he said.

I slid off my stool and looked through the cupboards till I found the canister of pepper hidden behind a box of trash bags. I tried to keep the seasonings all together in alphabetical order, but my mother or father was always messing them up.

My dad took the pepper and shook it over the pot. "So, how was the dance?"

"Fine," I said.

"Good."

End of conversation.

Unlike my mom, my dad seldom asked a lot of personal questions about my social life, and tonight I was glad.

"Chili powder," he said.

I finally found the chili powder in the drawer with the dish towels.

"You should invite her over for dinner," said my dad.

"Who?"

"That girl you took to the dance."

Since when had my dad become interested in hosting dinner parties?

"Kelly's parents are strict," I told him. "They don't allow her to eat with strangers."

My dad dropped several pounds of ground beef into the pot. "They sound like real screwballs," he said.

My mom was probably right about not telling my father. Even Superman couldn't expect me to drop a bombshell like this on my dad.

He lined up eight plump tomatoes on the cutting board and hacked them into tiny pieces.

After all, the only time I had ever heard him mention anything about homosexuals was when I was ten. He and a bunch of buddies from work were grilling brats in the backyard, drinking beer, and telling jokes. I was underneath the picnic table eavesdropping.

"Here's a good one," my dad had said. "How many fags does it take to screw in a lightbulb?"

No one had known the answer.

"Two. Unless it's a three-way."

I hadn't understood the joke, but I never forgot the laughter. How could I possibly tell a person like this I was gay?

He turned up the heat on the stove, and the chili began to bubble.

"So her folks won't let her eat over at our house, huh? I suppose we're not good enough for her. Take my advice, Steven. Don't get too serious about a girl like that."

He stirred the chili with a slotted spoon that looked suspiciously like the one he had used to scoop ice chunks out of our fishing holes.

"Remember, when you marry someone, you're marrying their entire family."

How did we get onto the topic of marriage?

"There are plenty of girls whose families will accept you just the way that you are."

But I wasn't looking for any girls.

"I want you to marry a woman who is proud to wear the DeNarski name, do you understand?" He brought down a cleaver with a resounding *whack!* and split a whole onion neatly in half.

"Dad, I'm gay."

I don't know who was more surprised, me or him.

"What did you say?"

"I'm gay."

Superman's X-ray vision was nothing compared with my dad's.

"Are you sure?"

I nodded.

He let out a long sigh, like air escaping from a beach ball. Then he rubbed a hairy-knuckled hand across his face and turned off the stove. "So, how old are you now? Sixteen?"

My stomach dropped. It was his turn to tell me that I was too young to be gay.

"I wasn't much older than you when I enlisted in the army."

Oh my God. My father was going to ship me off to the armed forces!

"It was a pretty big shock for a farm boy like me. I saw plenty of things I had never seen before. Like queers."

My mouth went dry.

"We even had a couple of them in my unit. Great big queers. And everyone knew they were queers too."

My mind raced with all the things that might happen to a couple of gay men in the army: court-martial, gang beating, lynching.

My father picked up the spoon, still dripping with chili. He pointed it at my head and spoke with the force of one who is not about to be contradicted.

"Those two men were some of the bravest, most decent guys I have ever known. Don't you ever in your life forget that, okay?"

I gulped.

"Got that?" he asked.

"Yes," I replied. "Yes, sir."

"Good. Now get me the salt." He turned back to the stove and resumed cooking.

On wobbly legs I began hunting for the salt. Did I really have this conversation with my dad, or had I been talking to a cleverly disguised impostor?

The salt wasn't with the silverware. It wasn't with the dish soap and bathroom cleaners either. It wasn't even in the bread box. At last I found it, alphabetized between the sage and the sesame seeds, exactly where it belonged.

My dad sprinkled a little into the chili, then took a taste. "Just one more thing," he said. "There's no reason to tell your mother about any of this. We'll keep it between you and me, all right? Just us two men."

CHAPTER
EIGHTEEN

My father knew I was gay. My mother knew I was gay. My best friend knew I was gay.

Too bad there wasn't anyone I could talk to.

I was afraid if I said anything more to Rachel, she'd organize a citywide demonstration, or nominate me for National Gay Student of the Year. My mom was still petrified by the topic. And my dad seemed to think that the matter was closed. It's on the table, we know the situation, no need to discuss it further.

But I did need to discuss it further. I might not be ready to be the founder and president of a gay/straight alliance at school, but I knew I was ready to talk to *somebody*. Somebody who could relate to the millions of emotions bouncing around in my head, ready to shoot out my ears. But where to find that somebody, I didn't know.

░ ░ ░ ░ ░ ░ ░ ░

I decided to try the Internet. For years I had been a frequent visitor to a chat room devoted to collectors of Superman memorabilia. Somewhere on the Web there had to be a similar site for kids like me who were cautiously creeping out of the closet.

I waited till there was an afternoon when both my parents were out of the house, then snuck into my mom's study and turned on her computer. A quick visit to Google uncovered a Web site that seemed tailor-made for me: LONELY GAY TEENS — TALK LIVE, NOW!

What more could I ask for? I was lonely, I was gay, and boy, did I want to talk.

I double-clicked the link and was whisked to a screen that asked for my nickname. Somehow "Geezer" didn't seem appropriate, so instead I chose something that reflected my interests but didn't make me sound quite so boring: Superman.

Maybe I'd hook up with another collector.

A bright pink triangle flashed on the screen and I was instructed to wait while being connected to other visitors. Then the screen turned a deep blue, and a message appeared at the bottom.

BIG DADDY: HEY SUPERMAN.

Big Daddy? Ha! And I had been worried that "Geezer" would sound weird!

I typed a reply and hit the return key.

SUPERMAN: HEY BIG DADDY.

His response was instantaneous.

BIG DADDY: WHAT ARE YOU WEARING?

I reread his question several times. It seemed a strange first thing to ask, but I gave him a quick rundown of what I had on.

SUPERMAN: WHITE SOCKS, A BLUE T-SHIRT, A SWEATSHIRT FROM MOUNT RUSHMORE, A STRIPED SWEATER, AN OLD PAIR OF JEANS.

No use pretending I was into high fashion when I wasn't.

BIG DADDY: SOUNDS HOT.

No, not really. My dad kept the thermostat at sixty-five, and everyone in our house has learned to dress in layers.

The guy was quick with another question.

BIG DADDY: WHAT DO YOU LIKE TO DO?

I thought about this carefully. Do I let this guy in on my secret hobby and risk sounding like a complete doofus, or do I play it cool and aloof? I chose the safe route and let him answer first.

SUPERMAN: LOTS OF THINGS. WHAT DO YOU LIKE TO DO?

And then Big Daddy told me.

I had thought Solveig Amundson was sexually uninhibited, but Big Daddy made her seem like Mother Teresa. Half the things he described didn't even sound physically possible.

"Hi, Steven, working on your homework?"

It was my mother, standing behind me with an armload of groceries.

I threw myself across the screen and hit the power switch in the back. With a tiny click, the computer's screen went dark. "Research," I blurted. "For biology."

"If you're done studying, you can help me carry in the rest of these bags."

She disappeared into the kitchen leaving me alone in her office with a blank computer and an exploding chest.

Big Daddy was gone.

And I was glad.

Don't get me wrong. I liked guys. I knew that for a fact. I liked the way their bodies looked. The thought of being physically close to one was exciting. And I wanted to be physically close to one too. But if I was going to be gay, did that mean I had to dive headfirst into the deep end of the sexual swimming pool?

Couldn't I just find somebody to *talk* to?

∎ ∎ ∎ ∎ ∎ ∎ ∎ ∎

"Nice hair."

"Thanks."

It was lunchtime, and I was eating with Rachel in the cafeteria. Her hair had been avocado green for almost a week.

"It's Victor's favorite color."

Victor and Rachel had been seeing a lot of each other. In the past week and a half they had gone to two movies and one Sierra Club meeting.

"But I'm not going to see him on Saturday afternoons or anytime during lunch," she had promised. "Those times will always be reserved for just you and me."

She dipped her fingers into a Tupperware container of guacamole and licked them clean one by one. Then she told me about a show she had watched on TV last night. It had nothing to do with the environment, disenfranchised minorities, or world peace. It was just a funny movie. Ever since she had been spending time with Victor, Rachel seemed a lot less serious. Playfulness looked good on her.

"You know, Steven, if you ever want to double-date again, just say the word."

"No thanks," I said. "Kelly and I have broken up."

Rachel licked the last of the guacamole off her thumb. "Not with Kelly. With a real date. An actual human being. Victor would be perfectly comfortable having you join us."

I shot her a quick, sharp look.

She crossed her heart and held up her hand. "I haven't told him anything. I swear."

"Well, thanks for the invitation," I said. "But I'm looking at a future of lifelong celibacy."

Rachel opened a bag of jelly beans and popped a yellow one into her mouth. She was even eating refined sugar now.

"That's too bad," she said, as she rolled the candy around on her tongue. "You're cute, Steven, and you're considerate too. You're also a lot of fun to be with."

Then she leaned forward and whispered so that no one else could hear. "Any guy in the world would be lucky to land a date with you."

A date? If I couldn't even find someone to talk to, where was I ever going to find a date?

I had forgotten my science folder in biology and when I swung by the room after school to pick it up, the door was locked. By the time I found a custodian to let me in, the buses had all left. Four phone calls home, and each time the line was busy, which left me walking.

It was sleeting out.

Fine. I was in a sleety mood.

A silver Grand Am sped past and splattered me with a shower of cold, slushy snow. Then it stopped, and backed up.

Was the sadistic driver going to drench me again?

The window on the driver's side slid open.

It was Mr. Bowman.

"My God, Steven. I'm sorry. I wasn't paying attention."

His face looked so upset that I was the one who wanted to apologize.

"Are you going home? Get in. I'll give you a ride."

He didn't have to offer twice.

I gave him my address and tossed my wet backpack onto the floor of his backseat. Then I sunk into the velvety upholstery of the front. I made a quick mental note: Forget folder in science on a regular basis.

"We've missed you at square dancing," he said.

I hadn't been back to the Bees since my date with Kelly. The Swensons would ask about the dance, and I couldn't bear to tell them I had opted for a dog over their granddaughter. "I'm taking a break," I said. "Giving my dancing shoes a rest."

"Fair enough," said Mr. Bowman.

I stole a look at his profile as he drove. It felt good being this close to him . . . and I didn't feel bad about feeling good.

"Are you coming to the game next week?" he asked. "If we win, we head to the state tournament."

I've never been to a high school hockey game in my life.

"Wouldn't miss it for the world," I told him.

"Terrific. In fact, I'm just making a quick stop at the district office, then it's back to school for practice."

We had already reached my house. I was sorry the trip was over so soon. "Thanks for the lift," I said.

"Anytime," he replied.

I reached behind me to get my pack, and that's when I saw it. Halfway hidden beneath the seat was a copy of *International Male.*

It was as if Christmas and my birthday had arrived at the same moment. Throw in a double dose of Thanksgiving as well. I had just found the person I could talk to, and his name was Tom Bowman.

CHAPTER NINETEEN

Okay, just because Mr. Bowman had a copy of *International Male* hidden in his car didn't make him gay. Maybe he just liked to dress well. Maybe he just liked to scout out the latest fishnet tank tops and micro-brief running shorts.

Yeah, right. And straight guys bought *Playboy* for the articles.

My next move was clear. I would catch Mr. Bowman tomorrow after hockey practice. I'd casually bring up the weather, the hockey team, the magazine I had seen lying in the back of his car, and before I knew it, I'd be spilling out my guts to him. And more important, Mr. Bowman would be telling me everything I wanted to know about being gay but was afraid to ask.

I don't think I slept more than ten minutes.

It was a study day in health class. I studied Mr. Bowman. As he moved up and down the aisles, he joked with students, pointed out a new haircut, complimented a kid on a well-done homework assignment. As always he was perfectly pleasant and agreeable. No wonder everyone liked him.

Maybe I'd become a teacher too. I could do my student teaching in Mr. Bowman's class. It was official now: Corcoran had taken an early retirement and wasn't returning, and Mr. Bowman was his permanent replacement. After I got my teaching license, maybe I'd get a job in the classroom next door.

Who knows, maybe Mr. Bowman and I could even share an apartment together. After a long day of teaching we'd come home from work and I'd cook us up a big pot of chili. We'd discuss our day at school, listen to a little Elton John, then retire to the comforts of our neatly organized, spotlessly clean bedroom.

Hey, it could happen.

Rachel noticed my good mood at lunch. "It's nice to see you smiling, Steven. You should do it more often."

"Don't worry," I told her. "I will."

When my last class of the day ended, I hurried to the school's hockey rink. Just last year the hockey stick plant had put up the cash to build a state-of-the-art, indoor ice arena connected directly to the school. Our computer lab might be outdated, but at least the kids at Beaver Lake had the best when it came to ice.

From my seat in the stands I watched the team go through their drills. As they practiced their precisely organized formations, it dawned on me that hockey was a lot like square dancing: It was all a matter of knowing your place and doing what was expected of you.

Even though he was only an assistant, Mr. Bowman was more animated than either of the two head coaches. He ran alongside the boards, shouting encouragement and congratulating the skaters on good hustle. I've never had good hustle in my life, but I was ready to lace up a pair of skates and join the guys on the ice.

Two hours later, when practice had ended, Head Coach Pangborn blew his whistle and the players gathered around him in a circle. This was the same Pangborn who had cringed at the sight of my bloody nose. Industrial Arts teacher, hockey coach . . . this guy's life must be one accident-injury form after another.

"You morons skated like crap!" he bellowed.

Even though he wasn't talking to me, the disgust in his voice made me want to crawl beneath my seat.

"Unless you want to get your asses kicked by Lake Asta on Saturday, you'd better start skating like men. When I looked out onto the ice today, I didn't see any men at all."

The hockey players hung their heads like scolded puppies. Even Dwayne and the Bull. I didn't realize it was possible for anyone the size of the Incredible Hulk to look so ashamed.

I waited for Mr. Bowman to speak up and tell Pangborn that these fine young men had been trying their best and that there was really no reason to get so upset. It was, after all, only a game. But Mr. Bowman stood off to the side, hands folded respectfully behind his back. I guess when you're still an assistant, you don't want to make the head coach look bad by contradicting him.

Pangborn's voice softened, but not much.

"But I have confidence in you. I know you can do this. I know that deep down inside, each of you really *are* men. And those Lake Asta Walleyes, they aren't men. You know what they are? They're a bunch of friggin' faggots. And a bunch of friggin' faggots don't stand a chance against a team of men."

The other head coach standing next to Pangborn laughed. A few of the guys on the hockey team laughed too.

That, I could handle. I've heard plenty of laughter when people at school talked about homos and fairies. What I couldn't handle was the fact that Mr. Bowman was laughing just as loud as anyone else.

Maybe even louder.

"Now hit the showers!" said Pangborn. "And come back tomorrow when you're ready to play some real hockey."

The players clomped down the rubber path that led to the locker room.

I didn't move. I couldn't.

The two head coaches followed the team, but Mr. Bowman stayed behind and began collecting towels and water bottles. Then he noticed me, sitting about twenty feet away. "Steven! What are you doing here?"

The surprise on his face was quickly replaced by his familiar smile.

"I was just leaving," I said.

He took a couple of steps in my direction. I stayed where I was. "Why don't you wait a few minutes and I'll give you a lift."

Was it only yesterday that he had driven me home? It seemed like years ago. "Thanks," I said. "But no thanks."

He gathered up a bag full of pucks and set them down on a bench.

"You're still coming to the game on Saturday, aren't you? We'll need all the fans we can get."

Why would I want to go to a hockey game? I hated hockey. It was stupid of me to have forgotten that. "I'll have to see," I told him. "I might be busy that night."

Mr. Bowman continued to clean up after the team. He was as neat as any follower of my mother's book. He even brushed off the paper drinking cups before tossing them into the trash. It dawned on me that it was possible to be *too* neat.

Suddenly I wanted to go home. Maybe even mess up my room a little.

As I walked toward the exit, Mr. Bowman called after me. "See you tomorrow, Steven."

I turned and gave him one more look. He was bending over, picking up a couple of hockey sticks. I don't know why I had never noticed this before, but there, on top of his head, was the unmistakable beginning of a bald spot.

How could I have ever thought that this guy looked like Superman?

* * * * * * * *

"You're home from school awfully late, Steven. Better not have a snack. It's almost time for dinner."

My mom was in the kitchen, following my father closely with a legal pad and taking notes as he made pork chops. Her *Clean Teen* book had gotten a glowing review in the *New York Times* and her publisher was pressuring her to finish her working woman's cookbook as soon as possible. My dad looked ready to bite somebody's arm off.

I didn't even say hi. I went to my room, closed the door, and quietly sat on my bed.

Okay, maybe Mr. Bowman wasn't gay. Or maybe he was. All I knew for sure was that he wasn't the guy I wanted to share an apartment with.

I kicked off my shoes and let them bang against the wall. I took off my jacket and threw it after them.

Then I spotted today's mail lying on the edge of my desk. Ever since I'd turned sixteen I had been the target of daily recruitment catalogs from the Navy, the Marines, and the Air Force. I was in no mood to read how the military could turn me into a real man, so I grabbed the stack and slammed it hard into my wastebasket. As I did, a hand-addressed envelope fell to the floor.

Beaver Lake postmark. No return address. Unfamiliar handwriting. Probably from the Coast Guard, trying to camouflage their latest recruitment plea. When I ripped open the back, the temperature in the room dropped twenty degrees.

It was one of Rachel's pink handouts for the gay/straight alliance.

Rachel had promised that she wouldn't show anyone these flyers until I was ready. Had she lied to me? For the second time that day, I felt betrayed.

There was nothing else inside the envelope, not even a Post-it note. I unfolded the wrinkled sheet, turned it over, and discovered the handwritten message on the back:

Dear Steven,

We've missed you at the Busy Bees. Mavis feels real bad that she might have scared you off with all her talk about Belinda. In case you're wondering, Belinda found a boyfriend. He's a trombone player in the marching band. Real nice, but not as nice as you.

By the way, this fell out of your pocket the last time we saw you. Thought it might be important. I was hoping to give it to you in person, but you haven't been around and I didn't know if I should send it home with your mom.

Hope to see you square dancing again.

Morris Swenson

P.S. Our grandson Phillip used to attend a group like this at the coffeehouse in Summerfield. Mavis said she'd like the two of you to go out for burgers sometime, except Phillip lives away at college now and doesn't get home much. That wife of mine never learns, does she?

■ ■ ■ ■ ■ ■ ■ ■

Eight times I dialed the phone number. Eight times I hung up. Finally, on the ninth try, I stayed on the line.

"Summerfield Coffeehouse. This is Sheila."

"Hi. I was wondering . . ."

"Yes?"

"When do you open?"

"Six A.M., seven days a week, thanks for calling—"

"Wait! I was also wondering . . . do you have organic green tea?"

It was Rachel's favorite drink. I tried it once and thought it tasted like grass clippings.

"Yes, we do."

"And do you serve sandwiches?"

"We bake our own bread every morning."

"And do you accept credit cards?"

"Yup."

I was running out of questions.

"And are there any groups that hold meetings there?"

"Sure. Plenty."

"Like what?"

In the background I heard plates rattling and someone calling for a mocha latte.

"Single Fathers, Fantasy War Gamers, Summerfield Knitting Circle . . ."

The whipping sound of the espresso machine almost drowned out her voice.

". . . Parents of Twins, Seniors Who Swing . . ."

Maybe the group that Mavis and Morris's grandson had attended no longer existed. Maybe it had disbanded due to lack of interest.

". . . Llama Ranchers of Minnesota, Gay and Lesbian Youth Group —"

"Gee," I said, interrupting her. "That last one — just out

of curiosity — not that I'm planning on attending or anything, but when do they meet?"

"The first Sunday of every month. One o'clock, upstairs."

The first Sunday of the month was this weekend.

I thanked Sheila six or seven times and promised that whenever I was in Summerfield, I'd be sure to stop by the coffeehouse and leave her an extra-big tip.

No, I still wasn't ready to make a public announcement on CNN, but attending a support group an hour's drive from home, where there was little chance that I'd run into anyone else that I knew . . . that sounded good. Very good.

Now all I had to do was figure out a way of getting there.

▪ ▪ ▪ ▪ ▪ ▪ ▪ ▪

"Mom, I need my license."

She was at her computer, typing away.

"It's going to be spring before you know it, Steven. In just a few short weeks you'll be able to ride your bike. Then, after a good solid three months of practice driving this summer, we'll have a serious discussion about whether you're ready to take your test again."

"But I need my driver's license now."

She swiveled around in her desk chair. "We've been through this before, Steven. We've seen what happens when you take your test prematurely. What could possibly be so important that you need to get your driver's license right this very minute?"

I took a deep breath. "I want to go to a gay youth group that meets in Summerfield. And I want to be able to drive there by myself."

The color fled from her face. The "later" when she had promised we'd talk about being gay, and which had resided so safely in the future, had finally arrived.

"Oh. I see."

She bit the bottom of her lip so hard that I thought she was going to chew a hole through the skin. "Isn't this rather sudden?"

"No, not really. I've been thinking about this for a long time."

Ever since yesterday, when I'd gotten the note from Morris and talked with Sheila at the coffeehouse.

"I've got a better idea," said my mom. "Why don't we go to the library and see if they have any movies about being gay? Didn't Tom Hanks win an Oscar for playing a homosexual? We could check the movie out and watch it together."

"I don't want to watch Tom Hanks, Mom. I want to talk with other people in person." Then I added, "Please. It's important to me."

From somewhere on her cluttered desktop my mother produced a large yellow paper clip. She began twisting it back and forth.

"Who exactly is going to be there?" she asked.

"Kids," I said. "Gay kids."

"And just what are these gay kids going to be doing?"

"It's a support group. They'll be supporting each other." At least that was my educated guess.

"There won't be any alcohol involved, will there? One drink can make a young person do all sorts of things that he'll regret for the rest of his life."

"It's at a coffeehouse, Mom. You don't get drunk on cappuccinos."

"Does it meet at night?" she asked. "I am not going to let you socialize with a group of total strangers after dark."

"It's at one in the afternoon."

She had now mangled the paper clip into an unrecognizable shape. "But Summerfield is so far away."

"It's only an hour's drive — on a smooth, straight road. I can do it, Mom. You know I can."

The paper clip snapped in two. She set the pieces on her desk and looked for something else she could mangle. She settled on squeezing the arms of her chair.

"I'll tell you what, Steven. I'll let you take your driving test one more time. If you pass, you can go to this group. If not, we'll look for a movie. If that isn't a reasonable offer, then I don't know what is."

CHAPTER TWENTY

As my mom and I sat in the waiting area, I wondered who my driving examiner would be this time. The Easter Bunny? My preschool teacher? An alien from the planet Pituku?

"DeNarski? You're next."

A young man with shoulder-length black hair and a wicked grin was standing at the door with a clipboard.

"Good luck," said my mother. "And remember, failing your driving test three times in a row is nothing to feel embarrassed about."

The examiner and I walked out to the car and climbed in. There was something sexy and familiar about this guy, especially around his dark eyes. Was he an actor? A rock star? A model from one of the underwear catalogs? His name badge said TONY, but that didn't help.

He looked at his clipboard, then gave me the once-over. "Say, aren't you the kid who took a golden retriever to the dance? My cousin Victor was telling me all about you."

Of course! How could I have missed the resemblance? No shortage of handsome genes in that family.

Remembering how Kelly and I had been the hit of the evening, I sat up a little straighter. I was now a semi-legend, recognized by gorgeous civil servants. "Yup," I said. "That was me."

Tony wagged his head. "Man. And I thought Victor was pulling my leg. I didn't think anyone was really that deranged."

With those words of confidence, my test began.

There's something to be said for taking your driver's test three times. I knew exactly what to expect. I stopped at all the right places. I only checked my mirrors twice before changing lanes. I even managed to parallel park an inch from the curb in three skillful moves. The entire test went as smoothly as a well-rehearsed promenade.

When Tony told me I could drive the car back to the exam building, I had to refrain from dancing in my seat. I had passed. I knew it. Even if he considered me a lunatic for dating a dog, there was no way he could give me a failing grade. He jotted a few final notes on his clipboard, then ripped off my copy of the test and held it out.

"Sorry, Dog Man. Better luck next time."

I felt my heart being torn from my chest and slammed down a mine shaft. When it hit the bottom, I looked at what Tony had written: 95 percent.

"Just kidding," he said, then laughed at his own clever joke.

A handsome face does not necessarily equal a good sense of humor.

When my mother discovered that I had passed my test and was actually going to this meeting, her worries multiplied exponentially. By Sunday morning, I thought she was going to need a sedative.

"Don't give your phone number out to anyone."

"Yes, Mom."

"Don't use the bathroom unless there's a lock on the door."

"Yes, Mom."

"Call if there's anything you need. I can be there in thirty minutes."

Getting to Summerfield in thirty minutes would require considerable speeding on her part, a clear indication of how panicked she felt.

"Everything is going to be fine," I told her.

"Are you sure you don't want me to go along?" She had followed me out to the car in her bedroom slippers and was standing in a pile of slush. "I'll just stay a few minutes, until you get a chance to meet some of the other kids."

"Mom, this isn't the first day of kindergarten."

"Well, it certainly feels like it."

She closed her eyes and took several calming breaths. She was doing her best, and I had to give her credit for that. When she opened her eyes again, her face looked a little more relaxed. "Can I at least give you a kiss good-bye?"

For some reason that made me laugh. "Sure."

She gave me a peck on the cheek and rearranged the hair I had spent an hour combing. "Now go and have fun," she told me. "I'll be waiting to hear all about it the moment you get home."

* * * * * * * *

It was a strange feeling being in the car by myself. I liked it. I turned the radio on full blast, something neither of my parents would have allowed. After about two blocks, I turned it off again. I don't like loud music. Instead, I recklessly rebelled against both my mom and dad and drove precisely the speed limit all the way to Summerfield.

The hour drive gave me plenty of time to continue with what I'd been thinking about all week. What would these other gay teenagers be like? Would they be like Big Daddy from the Internet: ready for sex and poised to pounce? Or would they be like the photo of teenagers I had glimpsed in Rachel's gay magazine: reserved, sophisticated, and witty-looking?

I pictured a room filled with young *GQ* models, all of

them holding fancy coffees and discussing great literature. The only great literature I had read this year was *The Great Gatsby*, which we were studying in English. I tried to remember the comments on the back of the book, and practiced making intelligent remarks.

"Oh, yes, I think *Gatsby* is a perfect metaphor for today's society, just as relevant now as when it was written."

On second thought, maybe I should keep my mouth shut and stick to smiling quietly.

The Summerfield Coffeehouse was located in the center of town, right alongside an old movie theater. They shared a roomy parking lot, but I drove down the block till I found two cars that I could parallel park between. Successfully demonstrating my driving skills gave me the confidence to go inside.

A bell jingled above the door as I entered. The place was packed with Sunday afternoon coffee drinkers sitting at tiny tables, reading the paper or laughing in groups of two and three. A jungle of philodendron vines drooped from the ceiling, and the air was mixed with the smells of cinnamon, chocolate, and freshly ground coffee beans.

And there, on the far side of the room, was the wooden stairway leading up to the second floor.

I sat down in an overstuffed armchair as far from the staircase as possible.

"Our flavor of the day is roasted hazelnut decaf."

A sleepy-looking college student in a Gumby T-shirt was standing over me, holding a small notepad in his hand. Shiny silver rings pierced his ear, nose, cheek, and lip, and a long silver chain connected them all before disappearing down the neck of his shirt.

"No thank you," I said. "I don't like coffee."

"We've got tea, Italian soda, fruit juice, and mineral water. Which do you want?"

"I'm not very thirsty."

"Brownie? Bagel? There's one slice of banana pumpkin bread left."

I picked up a copy of *Haiku Journal* from the table next to me.

"Actually, I just came here to read."

"Yeah, sure," said the waiter. He gestured with his notepad to the stairway. "The gay and lesbian group meets up there."

Before I could think of a snappy response, he was gone.

It was now or never. I stood, walked to the stairs, and began the climb. With each step my nervousness shrank and my excitement increased. So what if everyone else was more experienced or more sophisticated than I was? It didn't matter. I was finally going to meet some other gay guys my own age.

My head cleared the second-floor landing. I was looking into a large, open area lit by two sunny skylights. A garage sale assortment of chairs and tables was scattered about the room. The walls were painted with a mural of a colorful rain forest. And everywhere I looked, there were teenagers.

They were all girls.

Teenage girls playing Trivial Pursuit. Teenage girls watching an Ellen DeGeneres special on an old TV set. Teenage girls chatting with one another on a red satin couch. If it hadn't been for the GAY/LESBIAN/BISEXUAL/TRANSGENDER/ TRANSSEXUAL SAFE PLACE banner hanging from the ceiling, I would have thought I had walked into a Girl Scout reunion.

Had I gotten the date wrong? Did males and females alternate months? Or maybe . . . maybe there weren't any other gay guys in this part of the state.

A pair of girls politely excused themselves as they came up the stairs and edged their way around me.

"Lynne! Angie!"

The girls on the couch called them over. Soon they were laughing and joking with the others. I watched them and wilted.

Where were the other guys?

Where were the other guys who kept underwear magazines beneath their beds? Where were the other guys who had erotic dreams about their male teachers? Where were the other guys who someday, possibly, might want to double-date with me and Rachel and Victor?

Where were the other guys I could talk to?

Wherever they were, they certainly weren't here in this coffeehouse.

I wallowed in self-pity for several well-deserved minutes. Then I gave myself a kick. Figuratively, not literally.

So what? Who cared if there weren't any other guys? Gay girls could be just as supportive as gay boys, couldn't they? I had come all this way to meet other gay teenagers, and that was exactly what I was going to do.

I looked around the room and tried to find a group that might welcome a dull male square dancer. Who knows, maybe some of these girls had gay brothers. I saw a girl who looked a little like Rachel and was about to approach her, then froze. I spotted him. Another male. He was mostly hidden behind a brick pillar, but I could definitely tell he was male.

A jolt of electricity rushed to the ends of my fingers and toes. Thank you, thank you, oh gods of the coffeehouse!

He stepped forward and moved into view.

It was Dwayne Becker, from the hockey table.

The room began to tilt.

The testosterone king of the school was gay? Impossible. If Trent Beachum were here, he'd die.

Forget about Trent, *I* was going to die.

I knew it was rude, but I couldn't pry my eyes off him. How could Dwayne be gay? It was simply not within the realm of belief.

And then I thought, why not? Who says hockey players

can't be homosexuals? I had enjoyed a very brief career as a puckster myself way back in my younger days. Maybe his date with Solveig had been just an act. Been there, done that too. And I distinctly remembered that Dwayne had *not* laughed at Pangborn's stupid comments.

All the pieces were beginning to fit. Of course Dwayne was gay! Why hadn't I figured it out before?

Dwayne caught me staring and turned the other way. I had scared him. He probably didn't expect to run into somebody else that he knew. Well, neither had I.

We could have stood there on opposite sides of the room forever, but I was determined to meet another guy, and if that meant making the first move, so be it.

"Hey, Dwayne," I said, walking his way and showing my friendliest let's-get-acquainted smile.

Dwayne pretended not to hear.

"First time here?" I asked.

He folded his arms and looked at the ceiling.

"Yeah, mine too," I said.

Continued stony silence. Not exactly the warm, male-bonding experience I had hoped for, but maybe if I opened up a little, Dwayne would relax and start talking. "I don't know about you, but I was pretty nervous coming here. In fact, you're the first gay person I've ever met."

That finally loosened him up. "I'm not gay," he said.

Boy, was that a phrase I was familiar with.

"I know what you mean," I told him. "I said the same thing myself for a long, long time."

Dwayne put his hand over his face as if to hide. This guy was even more closeted than I was.

"Even if you can't say it, you took a big step in coming here. Congratulations. That took guts. Real guts. You should be proud of yourself."

It sounded like a pep talk that Rachel would give.

Dwayne growled from the back of his throat. "I'm not gay," he repeated.

"Take your time," I said. "But once you're ready to say it, you'll feel better. Believe me. I know."

Dwayne leaned over me and his head blocked the sun from the skylights.

"Are you deaf, Upchuck? I told you, I'm not gay."

"Dwayne!"

A tall, willowy woman with short hair and black jeans came bounding up the steps. She looked a little old to be a gay/lesbian/bisexual/transgender/transsexual youth, but who was to say what the age restrictions were?

She wrapped her arms around Dwayne as far as they would go and gave him a hug. "Sorry I wasn't here to meet you. I was talking on the phone, and the call took longer than I thought."

"Don't worry about it," said Dwayne. He reached into

his pocket and handed her a set of keys. "Thanks for letting us use the van. We'll meet you downstairs when the movie's over."

The woman clipped the keys to her belt. "Enjoy the show," she said. "And tell Solveig hi."

Dwayne was halfway across the room. He pulled his Marlboro cap from the pocket of his sweats and adjusted it on his head. "Thanks, Mom," he said, and was gone.

If it were possible to die of self-initiated spontaneous combustion, I would have been a smoldering pile of ashes on the floor.

"Hi!" said Dwayne's mother, turning her attention to me. "My name is Shari, and I'm one of the adult leaders here. And I bet I know what you're thinking. Yes, moms can be lesbians too."

That was the last thing I was thinking. I was thinking how many seconds it would take for Dwayne to call the hockey team and tell them I was gay.

"It's always great to see a new face," said Shari. "Let me take you around so you can meet some of the regulars."

She took my elbow and led me to the group of girls on the couch. They told me their names, but the only thing I heard was Dwayne repeating that he wasn't gay, and me insisting that he was.

"And this is Persephone," said Shari, introducing me to

a big-boned girl with a head full of dreadlocks. She smiled, and her mouth sparkled with braces.

"Lucky you," said Persephone. "I bet you didn't realize this was Lesbian Appreciation Day. All girls and no guys."

Was there really a holiday like that, or was she joking?

"We do seem to be short on fellows today," said Shari. "Where are they this month?"

Persephone counted on her fingers.

"Seth has a dentist appointment. The Jackson twins have to work. Mike Capella got stuck baby-sitting his sister, and the rest drove down to Minneapolis to see that new movie starring superstud Antonio-what's-his-name."

I bet Solveig would have loved superstud Antonio-what's-his-name. Why couldn't Dwayne have taken her to Minneapolis instead of showing up here in Summerfield?

"Cheer up," said Persephone, tugging on my sleeve. "Who needs guys anyway? You're going to have a good time with us girls. C'mon, you can be my partner for a little dyke Ping-Pong."

She rounded up a couple of friends and they cleared off an old, warped Ping-Pong table. The legs were wobbly, the ball was dented, and the paddles were cracked down the middle.

"We call it dyke Ping-Pong because the ball never goes straight."

Persephone and I were losing badly, 19 to 3, when Shari announced it was time to check in. The girls moved the furniture into one big circle and began telling about their past month. Some had new jobs. Some had been on vacation. Some had younger siblings that they wanted to auction off on eBay. They all had something funny or interesting to say.

And then it was my turn. Twenty-three teenage girls (I had counted) and one lesbian mother stared at me and waited for me to speak.

"My name is Steven," I said, but that was as far as I got. Here it was, my first statement to a group of kindred souls and my brain decided to take a time-out.

Shari and the girls waited patiently for me to continue. Maybe if I started moving my lips, something intelligent would spring forth.

"And I think *The Great Gatsby* is a perfect metaphor for today's society."

I swear it was the only thing I could think of.

Shari was at a loss to respond. "Oh. I see."

She looked around the group, hoping that one of the girls would jump in with an appropriately positive comment. No such luck. They were all staring at me like I had tentacles growing out of my ears.

"Is there anything else you'd like us to know?"

Considering my first remark, that was a brave thing to ask.

Finally one other thing popped into my head. "I passed my driver's test," I said. "Yesterday. On the third try."

For a moment, the room was quiet. Then every single girl stood up and cheered. Some even whistled.

"Way to go, Stevie!" said Persephone. "It took me five tries to nail that baby."

After that, everyone had driving horror stories they wanted to tell. One girl had backed over her instructor's foot. Another had received her first speeding ticket leaving the exam station. I never realized there were so many ways to embarrass yourself in a car.

Finally Shari clapped her hands and held up a video. "Who's in the mood for a movie?"

Good. We had finally come to the gay part of the meeting. Maybe this would be a movie that explained homosexual basics, like how to recognize other gay people, what to do if somebody sets you up with a date of the wrong sex, and how to salvage your life once the biggest jock at school discovers you're gay.

The video was *Finding Nemo*.

I hadn't realized that *Finding Nemo* was a gay movie. I watched it closely, looking for the hidden gay messages, but they remained beyond my grasp. The only gay thing I noticed were two girls on the couch holding hands.

I could have learned more watching Tom Hanks.

After the movie ended and everyone said how cute it was, the girls began to put on their coats and leave.

"Nice to meet you, Steven!"

"Congrats on your license!"

"That's it?" I asked Shari. "The meeting's over?"

She pointed to a clock on the wall. It was already after four.

"I hope you'll come back next month," she told me. "It was a real pleasure getting to know you."

I doubted whether her son would agree.

True to her word, my mother was waiting at the door when I got home. She was gripping the phone as if ready to call the police had I been any later. "So, what was it like? What did you do? How many kids were there?"

She pulled me into the living room and sat me down before I could even unzip my coat.

"It was fine," I said. "I had fun."

She studied my face and frowned. "You don't look like you had fun."

"I did," I said. "Honest."

And when I thought about it, it was true. All of the girls were nice. So was Shari. Even losing at dyke Ping-Pong was kind of fun.

"It's just that . . ."

My mother held her breath.

"I was the only guy there. Everyone else was a girl."

She tried to look sympathetic, but I could tell she was relieved.

"And somebody from school saw me. Somebody I didn't want to find out I was gay."

This time the sympathy was real. "Oh, Steven. I'm sorry."

We sat there on the couch for a while without saying anything.

Eventually my mother spoke. "How about if I bring you some cookies? I baked them while you were gone."

That explained why the house smelled so smoky.

"Sure," I said. "Why not."

She came back in with a bowl full of crispy black poker chips and two big glasses of milk.

"Do you know what I was thinking while I baked these?"

You were thinking that you and the oven made a lethal combination?

"I was thinking that you're a very brave young man."

She reached across the couch and held my hand. "And I was thinking how much I loved you."

She gave my hand a squeeze. "And I was also thinking how lucky I am to have a wonderful gay son who makes me so proud."

She picked up a cookie and rapped it against the side of the bowl. It sounded like concrete being hit with a hammer.

"And finally, I was thinking I used way too much oatmeal in this recipe. Or maybe not enough cornstarch."

I took the cookie from her hand and snapped off a corner between my teeth. Cornstarch or not, I thought it tasted delicious.

CHAPTER
TWENTY-ONE

W hen I got to school the next morning, I half-
expected to find a banner hanging over the
front doors:

ATTENTION, STUDENTS AND STAFF!
STEVEN DENARSKI IS A HOMOSEXUAL!

Dwayne had known I was gay for nearly a day. Surely the
word must have spread.

And in fact, there *was* a banner over the front doors. But
it had nothing to do with me. It was a huge banner congratulating the hockey team on winning their Saturday game.
Next stop, the state tournament.

The proclamation that bore my name was considerably

smaller. It was printed on a piece of recycled typing paper and taped directly above my locker:

CONGRATULATIONS TO BEAVER LAKE'S
NEWEST DRIVER,
STEVEN DENARSKI!
I KNEW YOU COULD DO IT!
LOVE, RACHEL

In my opinion, it looked fifty times better than anything the cheerleaders could have made.

Rachel's good wishes lifted my spirits, but I knew it was only a matter of time before I faced the fallout from my encounter with Dwayne. Snide looks? Name calling? My head stuck in the toilet and flushed? I didn't know what it would be, but I knew that something had to happen.

I waited for it to happen that morning.

It didn't.

I waited for it to happen at lunch.

It didn't.

But later that week, as I was hurrying to my second-hour class, I spotted Dwayne and two buddies coming at me from the other end of the hall. The three filled the hallway like an industrial-size snowplow.

I could have turned around or hidden in the bathroom,

but frankly I was tired of waiting. For that matter, I was tired of hiding too. So I just kept walking and aimed for the narrow opening between Dwayne and the wall.

As I reached the spot where Dwayne could have easily body-checked me into the lockers, I readied myself for whatever was going to happen next.

"Hey, Upchuck," he said.

"Hey, Dwayne," I replied.

And we passed.

That was it. He went his way; I went mine. I began breathing again when I got to my class.

I suppose I shouldn't have been surprised that Dwayne didn't give a rat's rear if I was gay. Like, duh, his own mother was a lesbian. But I *was* surprised, as well as profoundly relieved.

It's nice to discover that some surprises can be good ones.

■ ■ ■ ■ ■ ■ ■ ■

Before the day's end, Vice Principal Cheever made another of his all-school announcements on the classroom monitors. This time he was flanked by the two head hockey coaches and Mr. Bowman.

"I'd like to take this opportunity to congratulate our fine coaching staff on the outstanding job they're doing with this year's hockey team. We are proud to have dedicated teachers like these working at Beaver Lake."

Even when he had something positive to say, Cheever still sounded like he was delivering a eulogy.

Mr. Bowman spoke next. "Thank you for your kind words, Mr. Cheever, but all of the congratulations belong to the team. They are the ones who worked their tails off and earned this trip to the state tournament. They are the ones who deserve our praise."

He then went on to recite the entire roster of players from memory.

The guy had class, you couldn't deny it. And he still looked pretty good in a designer shirt.

On the bus ride home I began to work out the math: 24 more days until the next support group; 576 hours; 34,560 minutes. Calculating the exact number of seconds seemed a little obsessive, even for me.

My mother asked about school. My father made a tuna noodle hot dish for dinner. All in all, it was an ordinary evening in the life of a slightly neurotic gay teenager.

Except something kept buzzing around in the back of my brain, just out of reach. Something that Mr. Bowman had said at the end of the day. And while it was annoying, it couldn't be very important, could it? All he had done was recite the list of hockey players.

Then, just as I was unloading the last butter knife from the dishwasher, it came to me.

Mike Capella.

He was one of the hockey players Mr. Bowman had named. He was also the guy Persephone had said was baby-sitting on Sunday.

Coincidence? Most likely. There were probably dozens of Capellas within a hundred miles of Summerfield.

Actually, there was only one. I had run to the phone directory and checked.

Okay. So maybe these two Mikes were one and the same. Maybe there really was another gay student at school. I'd find out for certain soon enough. There were only twenty-four days until the next coffeehouse meeting.

Unless Mike had to baby-sit again. Or my parents wouldn't let me use the car. Or a glacier broke lose from the polar ice cap and ripped a chasm through the center of the United States.

I picked up the phone and started dialing. It's what Rachel would have wanted me to do.

More important, it's what *I* wanted me to do.

Someone answered on the third ring.

"Is Mike Capella there?"

"Speaking."

"The same Mike Capella who had to baby-sit his sister last Sunday?"

"Yeah. Why?"

This was good, but not good enough. I had been fooled once by Dwayne and I wasn't about to be fooled again.

"The same Mike Capella who also happens to be gay?"

Silence.

What a stupid thing to have asked. Of course this guy wasn't going to say yes. Even if it were true, why would anyone admit this to a total stranger?

"Damn right I'm gay. Who the hell wants to know?"

Being sworn at had never felt so good.

"My name is Steven DeNarski, I go to your school, and I happen to be gay too." The words rushed out of my mouth like prisoners making a jailbreak.

Another pause. This time a little longer.

"Okay," said Mike. "That's cool."

And since I was already speeding down this highway of irrational bravery, I decided to throw out the brakes and hit the accelerator. "And I was wondering if you'd like to get together sometime. To talk."

"Do I even know you?" asked Mike.

Wham! I had crashed into a brick wall. I was afraid it was going to come to this.

"Sort of," I said. The words were no longer in such a hurry to escape. "I used to sit at the hockey table, in lunch. I was the quiet one, at the end."

I squeezed my eyes shut and waited for his reaction when he finally realized who I was.

"Cool," he said. "Very cool."

"Cool" was rapidly becoming my favorite word.

Fueled by one more burst of adrenaline, I continued. "So how about this weekend?" I asked.

"Can't," said Mike. "I've got hockey."

Of course he had hockey. It was the state tournament. Unless he was using hockey as an excuse not to meet.

"What about Monday?" he asked.

Anyone with half a brain would have said yes.

I almost did.

"Can't," I said. "I've got square dancing. What about Tuesday?"

Not even a pause.

"Tuesday works for me."

"Cool."

My mind was pounding with a thousand questions I wanted to ask him: Did he know of any other gay kids at school? Did the hockey team know that he was gay? Did they really get to throw Mr. Bowman in the showers when they won their last game?

Good questions one and all. But they'd have to wait till Tuesday. Right now I needed to cement the details before my courage deserted me or Mike changed his mind. "Five-thirty? At the Pizza Barn?"

Long, long pause.

I had blown it. My comment about square dancing had finally sunk in.

"There's just one problem," said Mike. "I can't drive. My

dad won't let me get my license until I'm a senior. Pretty sick, huh?"

Man, were we going to have a lot to talk about.

"No problem," I said with the worldly air of one who has had his license for nearly a week. "I'll pick you up."

I got his address and wished him luck at the tournament. When he hung up, I collapsed exhausted onto the carpet.

A miracle. A genuine, modern miracle.

⸻

There was only one minor detail left to take care of.

"Mom, Dad, can I borrow the car?"

My dad was behind his newspaper and my mom was sitting on the floor, organizing the chapters in her new book. "Going somewhere with Rachel?" she asked.

"No," I said. "I'm going out for pizza, next Tuesday, with a guy from school." And then, just to make sure they heard correctly, I raised my voice and added, "He's gay."

My dad lowered his paper and my mom dropped the chapter she was holding. They exchanged quick looks, then turned toward me.

"Make sure you fill the tank," my dad said, and went back to reading.

My mother wasn't so calm.

"Are you sure you wouldn't rather invite your friend over here? We could all have pizza together and then play cribbage or rummy. Everyone likes rummy. I bet your father would make some of his famous mozzarella sticks. And I could whip up a big box of pudding for dessert."

When she saw that I wasn't interested in mozzarella sticks and pudding, she sighed. "All right. As long as you're home by eight. No, make that seven-thirty."

No self-respecting sixteen-year-old has to be home by seven-thirty on a weeknight, but I didn't argue. Not this time.

As I returned to my room to call Rachel and tell her the good news, I realized that she would want to know which of the hockey players was Mike. Come to think of it, so did I. In all my weeks of sitting at their table, I had never once heard anyone being called by that name.

Thank goodness for yearbooks. I flipped through the pages and found Mike Capella among last year's sophomores. I recognized him immediately. Mike Capella. Carp. The human garbage disposal. He was the guy who had drained the milk carton stuffed with food scraps.

My stomach began to feel queasy in remembrance.

What if Mike tried to do something like that again at the restaurant? What if I got sick? What if I got sick right on the pizza?

Once the fears started, they wouldn't quit.

What if someone from school saw us together? Would they know we were gay? Was this a date? And if so, was I supposed to pay? What if Mike wasn't gay after all, and this was actually an elaborate hoax staged by some awful reality show and I was being filmed by hidden cameras at this very instant?

I dropped to my bed and looked at the Superman poster on the ceiling.

Why were there always so many things to worry about?

Then I remembered Mike's nice smile when he had won the chugging contest. I remembered his friendly eyes. Slowly the worries began to quiet down. They didn't go away completely, but they took a backseat to another feeling: happiness.

No, I wasn't feeling happy. I was feeling something more than that.

I picked up the phone and dialed Rachel's number.

I was feeling absolutely, positively gay.

WANTED:
New dad, new life...
and a really great taco.

Meet Maybelline "Maybe" Chestnut. Her mom owns a charm
school in Florida, and her dad? Well, she doesn't know what he
does—or even who he is. So Maybe sets out on a quest to find
him—and much more—in faraway California.

ARTHUR A. LEVINE BOOKS

▲ SCHOLASTIC

www.scholastic.com

MAYB